A Step Too Far

Tony McFadden

DEDICATION

For Readers, everywhere.

You keep consuming and I'll keep creating.

ACKNOWLEDGMENTS

Many thanks to my writer friends at the fantastic
Northern Beaches Writers' Group.
Your feedback was immensely helpful.

Chapter One

Jesus, but it was hot. Like two rats fucking in a wool sock, hot.

Some strange meteorological thing was pushing hot air down the coast. It was over 40C, not a single cloud in the sky, with a wind that felt like a blast furnace. An early summer heat wave that was going to kill us all. It was preparing me for hell.

Lincoln sprinted down Budgewoi Beach, chasing a seagull. I wasn't going to run after him. He'd be back after chatting with a couple of Huskies and a Chocolate Lab. If I was lucky, he'd take a dump while he was down the other end of the beach, and I "wouldn't see it".

A young lady was kite surfing, kicking off the

top of the swells like a seasoned pro. She navigated closer to the shore, dropped the kite on the beach and rode the board in. As she got closer, I recognised the smile on her face. The last time I saw Jessie was at Jimmy's funeral four months ago. Her father told me she'd gone to Brissie to spend time with her aunt. I guess she was back.

Lincoln acted like he recognised her, too. But he'd never met her. That dog would run up to anyone he encountered, arse-end wagging like the person was a long-lost best friend. Jessie squatted down, and he knocked her into the surf and started playing with her.

She laughed and struggled under his weight, finally getting her butt on the sand. Linc sat beside her and let her pat him. She looked up as I approached. "Hey there, Mac. This your dog? I love Border Collies. How old is he?"

"Almost three. His name is Lincoln. When'd you get back?"

She scratched Linc under the ears. "Ooo, Linky-poo. You're cute."

Christ. Why does every female who meets Lincoln call him that? As if getting his nuts cut off wasn't emasculating enough. "Welcome back. You're looking good. You must have needed the break."

She looked up at me and slowly got to her feet. "Thanks." She gave me a hug. A tight one. "I really appreciate what you did."

"What did I do?"

She released me and took my hands. "You got the guy who killed Jimmy."

I grimaced and leaned down to attach the lead to Linc's collar. "Yeah, about that."

"I know people thought I wouldn't give him the time of day, but he was growing on me. He looked so sweet in his Security Guard uniform. And he wasn't always wanting to get on the piss."

Her eyes welled with tears. "I didn't leave until after the funeral. I was still here when Jackson was arrested. And he was arrested based on what you told the police. So, thanks." She gathered the leads to the kite and stuffed the contraption into a carry bag.

I slung it over my shoulder. Distant pain echoes of broken ribs rippled down my right side. Healing takes longer when you're old. "So, how long have you been back?"

"Just got in yesterday. It was the first surf in months. It felt good. My aunt kinda babied me up in Brissie." She picked up the short board and tucked it under her arm, and we walked side by side, Linc pulling my arm out of its socket every other lunge.

"Have you talked much about Jimmy or Jackson's arrest with anyone back here while you were away?"

She shook her head. "Avoiding *that* subject like the plague. Why?"

A timber 'sidewalk' took us from the beach over the dunes and to the parking lot. Most of it was a trap. Some council genius laid planks edge-wise in the sand and anchored them somehow. Half the planks were buried under the sand and waited to attack my toes, usually when I thought I was looking cool. Lincoln ran ahead, extending the retractable lead to its maximum. His toenails needed clipping. The clicking drove thoughts out of my head. I didn't know how to broach the subject.

Turned out I didn't have to.

We crested the dune and continued the walk down to the parking lot. A cop car was parked sideways across two spaces in front of the beach burger joint. The driver's door opened, and Senior Constable Will Grange pushed himself out and adjusted his belt. Grange is a good guy, I guess. A bit pompous. Whatever he wore, wherever and whenever, always looked freshly pressed and impeccable. He had his hair slicked back like an extra in The Sopranos and swaggered a bit more than was justified, but generally, he was a fair guy.

The passenger's door opened, and an overweight, greasy arsehole in cargo shorts, a dirty singlet and $5 thongs from K-Mart oozed out.

Jessie stopped. "Jesus. Is that...?"

I nodded. "Jackson. Not in jail. Sorry. I thought maybe you knew."

We had stopped walking. Like Jackson had some sort of repulsive force that kept us from getting closer. Lincoln tugged at the end of his lead, snapping me out of my reverie. "Let's go. Ignore him."

Jackson turned and started saying something to Grange when Jessie dropped her board and ran down the rest of the boardwalk, accelerating into a full-body slam. Jackson took the full force of her momentum, driving him into the car. He exhaled a grunt, fell to the pavement, and curled into a ball.

I dropped the kite bag and rushed in. She was driving her heel into his ribs and back repeatedly when Grange and I both reached her. I dodged a swinging foot, grabbed her around the waist, and lifted her back.

Grange leaned down and helped Jackson to his feet. Then grabbed him to arrest *his* lunge at Jessie.

It looked like a slapstick routine. I was holding back a lithe, extremely fit nineteen-year-old and Grange was holding back an overweight, greasy man in his fifties. Lincoln was barking his fool head off, running around us like he was trying to gather sheep.

I was tempted to let Jessie go, and if there hadn't been a cop present, I probably would have. Jackson wouldn't have had a chance.

She continued to struggle against my grip. I whispered in her ear. "Ease up, Jess. You can't win this. Even if you do."

She took a deep breath and relaxed.

"You going to behave?"

She looked over her shoulder at me. If looks. "For now. Let me go."

"If you attack Jackson again, Grange will arrest you."

"Okay, fine."

I have yet to hear a woman say 'fine' and have it mean 'fine'. I eased off on my grip, keeping a hand close. I didn't want her locked up. But I did want to see Jackson get the shit kicked out of him.

Jackson settled a bit, too. I don't know what Grange said to him, but he was brushing dirt off his T-shirt and sniffing. Deviated septum, I bet. Too much coke. Allegedly.

I pointed at him. "We good here, Jackson?"

"I am. You're a piece of shit. And that tramp needs to watch what she's doing. I'll let it go for now, but if I see her again, I'm not responsible for what I might do."

I grabbed Jessie's wrist before she had a chance to react. "Easy, Jess. Don't let him gee you up."

She relaxed, and I let go of her arm. She shook her head and walked back to pick up her board. "Fuck you, Jackson. Fuck off and die. The next time I see you, Mac won't be around to protect you. I'll finish you."

I took a step toward Jackson. "She doesn't like

you. Nobody does. You don't have many friends around here anymore. Why don't you piss off out west? The mines, maybe. You'll fit right in."

Half his face smiled. "Fuck off, Mac." He walked toward the food counter. "You buying me a burger, Grange?""

I'd been dismissed.

I scooped the bag of kite and caught up to Jessie in the parking lot, Lincoln happily trotting along beside me. Jess had a look on her face that put a stop to any questions. So I didn't ask any. She stuffed the board into a carry case and placed it on her car.

She strapped the board to the roof in silence while I stashed the bag in her back seat. "You okay?"

She glared at me, got in the car and started it. I leaned in the window. "I don't know the details. He's out of jail. Some deal he did, I think." I shrugged and added like it would make any difference to her, "He's off the force, though."

"He killed Jimmy. And he's walking around. What fucking good are you?"

The little car threw gravel off its front wheels as she hurriedly left. And she wasn't wrong.

Jackson was arrested, but before it got to trial, something happened, and he was back out. Kicked off the force, but a free man, nonetheless. The bank manager behind the robbery, Harris, was in for seven years, but Jackson, the guy who I actually saw kill someone, walked.

Grange and Jackson sat at one of the wooden picnic tables by the food counters. Even out of uniform, Jackson exuded 'officious bully'. He'd grown a moustache and the greasy hair was a lot greyer and thinner than it was four months ago. But the food behind bars must have been appealing. He was larger, if possible. A slice of hairy gut stuck out between the bottom of his too-small T-shirt and his cargo shorts. I doubt he could see his dick without a mirror on a stick.

Grange nodded at something Jackson said and picked at his chips. I walked over. I had to say something.

Jackson looked up at me as I approached, then ignored me, continuing his conversation with Grange. "So, Willy, they couldn't make it stick. Tainted evidence or something."

I slid onto the bench beside Grange, across

from Jackson. "You're letting this killer call you by your first name, Grange? Shouldn't he be calling you, at the very least, 'Senior Constable Grange, sir'? The guy is scum."

Grange rubbed the side of his nose with his index finger, then held his hand out to stop Jackson from speaking. He half smiled. "We're all people, Mac. Jackson's an old friend. The court determined there wasn't enough evidence to convict. Who am I to argue with the court?"

I looked at the two of them. Shook my head. "I like you, Grange. You've always been a good cop. Don't let this piece of runny shit ruin you."

Jackson took a sip of soda from his paper cup, mouthed "Fuck you" and flung the cup at me. My reaction has slowed a bit in my advancing years; at least, that's what I put the ice cube in the eye down to. I launched over the table and swung a right at Jackson's face, but he anticipated my lunge and slid to one side. I missed and ended up in a pile on the deck. I rolled and just avoided a kick to the kidneys. I scuttled a few metres away and stood, brushing sand off my ass.

Jackson wheezed and held his fists up, like

some old timey boxer.

"You're shitting me, right?" I laughed and wiped soda off my shirt. "You're as fit as my grandpa." I lunged forward, slapped his face and stepped back, hands up, loose and ready to shove the fat fuck's head up his arse.

"Jesus Christ. Stop it before I arrest both of you for being fucking idiots." Grange wiped soda off his shirt and swore. "Look what the fuck you did, Jackson." He unbuttoned it and shrugged it off. "Calm the fuck down."

He was wearing a singlet under his shirt. It was forty-something degrees out, and he was wearing an undershirt. And he had a spare shirt, of course. He tossed the dirty shirt in the back seat and pulled out a fresh one, folded like it had just come from a laundry service, and pulled it on, covering a bit of ink on his shoulder.

"I thought you were a clean skin, Grange. Let's see the ink." I ignored wheezy Jackson and walked to the other side of Grange's car. "What is it?"

He continued buttoning his shirt, loosening his belt, opening his pants and tucking the shirt in well.

"Are you two going to be okay? Or do we have a problem?"

I nodded. "Okay. Don't tell me. We're good. Catch you later, Grange." I pointed at Jackson. "You don't have a badge protecting you anymore. Cross the street when you see me coming."

I sighed and slid into my beat-up Corolla. Too hot. I sat halfway out of the car, and Lincoln hopped across my lap into the front passenger seat and leaned his head out the window. Oh, to have the life of a dog.

I pulled my door shut, turned the key in the ignition and offered up a silent prayer to the technology gods. It turned over rough three or four times before it caught. I had to do something about that.

Chapter Two

Jackson out on the street was burning me almost as much as it seemed to be burning Jessie. I parked outside my apartment/office and sat in the car for a minute. Still working out of the place I lived. Would be for some time, until business picked up.

Linc whimpered. The inside of my car felt like an oven inside of an oven.

"All right, all right."

We stepped into the heat. The asphalt felt soft underfoot, and the humidity was stifling. Thirty-seven steps straight up the outside of the building to my place, above the TAB. Like an alcoholic living above a pub.

The air conditioning strained in the apartment. I closed the door behind Lincoln quickly, and we both stood in front of the vent, soaking as much cold as we could. And it wasn't much. The air conditioning unit was on my list of potential future expenses.

Sophie came out of our bedroom with a suitcase and a pissed-off look. She wore a floral sundress and sandals, and her dark hair was pulled back in a sensible ponytail. She looked great. And pissed off. I ran through the last twenty-four hours in my head, ticking several things off the list that I knew she *didn't* know about. I couldn't think of a thing that she *did* know about that would put her in that mood.

I smiled at her. "So, where you off to?"

She stopped. Took a deep breath and pivoted toward me. "Don't get me started."

What the fuck did I do? "Ya know, Soph, you actually need to tell me what's going on. My telepathic skills kinda waned the day you moved in."

Her eyes narrowed. "My sister's husband—soon to be ex-husband—has followed his dick to the Gold Coast with the company's CFO. She's ten years older than my sister. *Older*. Can you imagine what that must feel like? The guy you married, whose underwear you washed, dumps you for someone ten years older than you? No. No, you can't. Because you're an arsehole male like every other arsehole male on the planet."

Great time to keep my mouth shut. I nodded and turned back to the cold air. Which, apparently, was *not* the right thing to do.

"Are you ignoring me?"

"I'm trying to figure out what it is I should do. Yes, Larry is a dick. Poor Gwen probably feels poorly, but ultimately, she'll be better off without him. I don't know either of them well, though, so I'm just guessing about all of this." I stayed facing the cold air, but the sweat was building on my forehead. "Is your brother heading up there, too?"

Her face clouded. "Stan? Another arsehole male." She sighed. "Haven't talked to him, or about him, since he was arrested. No interest in starting now."

"Sorry I asked. Go visit Gwen and get her head sorted. Get *your* head sorted. Just remember, when you're ready to come back, this arsehole male will still be here."

She released her hold of the suitcase handle and walked over beside Lincoln and me. "Fair enough. I'm a bit on edge. Gwen is my baby sister, and when she hurts, I hurt." She scratched Lincoln on the top of his head and leaned against me. "How was the walk this morning?"

I looked down at Lincoln, who was looking up at me, tongue lolling out of his mouth and a big doggie smile on his face. "Eventful. Ran into Jessie."

"She's back? Good for her. She needed a break after that mess with Jimmy. Does she seem like she's gotten over it?"

I sighed. "Yeah, she does. And then she found out that Jackson was out of jail. We ran into him at Budgie." I chuckled, remembering. "She fucking near killed him."

"My money would have been on Jessie. I miss all the fun." Sophie shook her head. "How did Jackson get out, anyway? He stole four and a half million from the bank, and you saw him shoot two people. Should buy him at least ten years in prison."

I nodded. "Beats the hell out of me how he got himself sprung. Hopefully, he doesn't hang around, or Jess really will kill him." I looked at her suitcase. "So, how long are you going to be in Newcastle?"

She shrugged. "As long as it takes." She squinted and looked up at me. "What is it with you men and commitment? I mean, they were what I thought was the perfect couple. Seemed to fit together perfectly." She took the suitcase handle. "At least they don't have kids. I'll call when I get there. Get used to cooking for yourself again."

The door kinda slammed behind her. Not really slammed like she's done in the past. More like when she's pissed but acknowledges that it's not *me* she's pissed at, just life in general. I looked at Lincoln who looked back up at me, a quizzical look on his face. Or he was hungry. Hard to tell with a dog.

"Well, pooch, it's back to you and me. For a little while, anyway." I took a deep breath and pulled an ice tray from the freezer. "Drink?"

I dropped half of the cubes into a large glass and the rest into his water bowl. Filled his up with water and mine with soda water and a couple of slices of lemon. What I wouldn't do for a beer, but I had a couple of kilos too many around the waist. My knees were starting to hurt with the extra weight.

I sat in front of the air-conditioning, soaking up the cold air for a minute. Lincoln finished at the water bowl and stretched out on the floor beside me. I looked down at him. "Buddy, I don't think I can handle bumping into that fat fuck on a regular basis. One of us is going to have to leave, and I'll be damned if it's going to be me."

The dog had a quizzical look on his face.

"I know. I've got no idea how to get him to leave town other than threatening physical harm, and I'm not that stupid." I downed the remaining bit of my drink and belched. "Let's go see what it's going to take to fix that car."

I stood and picked up the car keys from the table near the door. Lincoln was in full alert mode, practically wetting himself with excitement. "Jesus, dog. Calm down. It's just a drive."

Chapter Three

The dealership wouldn't even look at my piece of crap car for under $700. And it was getting harder to start.

But there was still Sally. She owned a smash repair joint north of town, and she had a couple of half-decent mechanics working for her. I was almost positive it was just spark plugs, and if I had the tools, I would have fixed it myself. But she'd do it for $100 plus parts—cheaper than paying for the wrenches. And honestly, I wouldn't know how to check the plugs.

Old friends from when I was on the force would shit themselves if they knew I was keeping Sally in business. I put her away a couple of times for minor drug charges, and over half of her 'staff' were frequent visitors at the station. Her husband, Hank, was currently three years into a twelve-year sentence for importing precursors. But she did a good job and was relatively inexpensive. I haven't caught her trying to rip me off. Yet.

I rolled to a stop and left the engine running with the air on full. I didn't want to have to attempt re-starting it if Sally didn't have time for me. Linc settled down on the front passenger seat, face in front of the cold air coming out of the vent.

Her place looked deceptive. From the street, it looked like a half-decent blow would flatten the garage. The tin roof and aluminium siding flapped when it got windy. Up close told a different story. They could barricade themselves in. It was virtually impenetrable. I know this from experience.

Sal was at the counter. "Hey, Mac, what can I do you for?"

"Keeping your nose clean?"

"You're not a cop any more, Mac. Fuck off."

I smiled. "Point taken. Can you fit my car in today? It's a bitch to start. And getting harder every day."

She looked past me onto the street. "You're still driving that piece of shit? I don't know if we've got parts that old."

"Probably just the plugs. It's been a long, long time."

Dick Backney came through the door from the garage wiping his hands with a dirty cloth. He stood almost two metres tall and was hard. He got away with the singlet look better than most. Certainly better than Grange.

His shoulders were the size of basketballs and his biceps rivalled my thighs. Both arms were inked from his wrists up, with a blue-ringed octopus on his right shoulder and a skull with a rose in its teeth on the left.

I like good ink, but not keen on doing it to myself. Some of his was quality stuff, but good portions of both sleeves were the product of prison ink. Pretty crude and as a result, menacing.

He tucked the cloth in his back pocket and completely ignored my presence in the room. "Hey, Sal, some fucknut left their car running in the drive. Blocking me in. I'm going to drive it into the bush."

He looked at me, then back at Sal. "That okay with you?"

"Bring it in and have a look at it. Mac says it's hard to start. He thinks it might be the plugs. Give it a good once over, okay?"

Dick looked at Sal for a moment, then at me. He didn't look much like a guy too concerned with customer service.

I smiled at him and nodded. "Let me get Lincoln out of it first. Thanks, Sally. How long do you think it'll be?"

She looked at Dick and had some sort of silent communication with him. She nodded and answered. "Come back at the end of the day. Should be right by then. Need a ride in?"

"Thanks, and no. The dog needs a walk. It's not that far. And I could use the exercise."

"Bring the poor dog in here out of the heat."

Lincoln was great chick-bait. If I weren't already tied up with Sophie, I'd be pulling like crazy. "Sure thing."

I clipped the lead on Linc and surrendered the car to Dick. The car sank on its suspension when he got in. None of his weight was fat.

Lincoln jumped up on Sally, his paws on her tits, as soon as he ran into the garage. I winced, expecting the kind of response *I'd* get of I tried that, but she was cool. Lucky mutt.

"What a gorgeous dog. What's his name?"

"Lincoln. Down, boy."

"Linky-poo. What a sweetie."

Jesus. This was uncharacteristic for Sally. Like the Queen breakdancing. "You okay, Sally? Heat's not getting to you, is it?"

She lifted Lincoln's paws off her chest, lowered him to the ground and scratched him behind the ears. "I love dogs, Mac. Don't trust anyone who doesn't."

Dick poked his head in from the work area, and I had to grab Lincoln by the collar before he lunged to see him, too. He looked at the dog, then at Sal. Completely ignored me. "It's a piece of shit. You sure it's just the plugs?"

"Find out why it's starting hard and fix that. Leave the rest."

"New plugs in the piece of shit will double its value." He still didn't look at me.

"Just do it, Dick." She turned away, dismissing him and crouched down to Lincoln's eye level. "How old?"

"Three. Ish. Rescue dog. Not positive of his birthdate, but we give him cake every July 1st."

"So he got a reprieve. That's nice." She frowned. "How did Jackson get his?"

"Don't know. Don't care. My preference would be that he was still behind bars." I shrugged. "Not that I get any say in the matter. Justice is blind." I scooped the end of Lincoln's lead off the floor. "Give me a call when it's finished, Sal. Don't gouge me too much, okay?" I dropped a business card on the counter.

"Can I call a taxi for you? It's pretty fucking hot out there today."

I'd be waiting for hours. "No, that's okay. Only a couple of klicks to walk." I patted my stomach. "Like I said, I could use the exercise."

"Sophie can't give you a lift?"

"In Newcastle. She's helping her sister out with a problem. She'll be gone for a couple of weeks."

Sally smiled. "Batching it, then? If you need any

company, let me know. I know some girls."

"Right. She'd have my nuts. No thanks, Sal. I'm an honest man now."

"Let me know if that changes, hun."

I grunted and left the garage. It had gotten hotter if that was possible. I regretted passing on the cab almost immediately. And while it really was only a couple of kilometres back to my place, there was not a hell of a lot of shade along the way.

I was dying in the heat, and I didn't have the fur Lincoln had. It was about five minutes into the walk, and I was about to turn back, for Linc's sake—I was fine, really—when a blue Mazda pulled up beside me and the passenger's window rolled down.

I leaned in the window and smiled at Ernie. I was going to get him to change his name to Earnie, since a good portion of my revenues recently have been me covering his ass for him. "Ern, mate, which way you heading?"

"Hop in. I'll give you a lift. Need you to help me out."

Excellent. Some business and air conditioning. I opened the back door and let Lincoln jump in and slid into the front seat. Lincoln stood with his back legs on the back seat and his front legs on the centre console and started licking Ernie's ear.

"Jesus Christ, Mac. Stop the fucking mutt, or I'll boot you both out."

I laughed. Lincoln loved everybody. As far as I could remember, he'd never met Ernie before, but they were, as far as Linc was concerned, best of friends.

I gave him a gentle push to the backseat. "Sit, Linc. Take it easy." Ernie wiped dog slobber off the side of his head, looking even more like Peter Lorre than usual. "What's it you want me to do, Ern?"

He pulled away from the shoulder and eased into traffic. The air conditioning was nice. I adjusted one of the dash vents to blast on my face and looked at him. "Is Betty giving you trouble?"

He drove in silence for a few seconds. "I'm trying to find her."

"She's left you?"

He shook his head. A little too hard. "She didn't say anything. She wasn't home when I got back from work yesterday. And she left her phone behind."

"Checked her friends?"

"I'm not an idiot." He pulled a file folder from between his seat and the centre console and handed it to me. "All of her information is in here. Let's talk about it at your office. I need a drink."

The folder was filled with bank statements, computer credentials, and photos of various forms of ID. I handed it back to him. "I know what she looks like. She's been in my office often enough."

He looked at me a bit too long.

"Eyes on the road, mate."

He swivelled to front and centre. "She *has* been to your office often enough. I've fucked up, haven't I? I screwed around on her too much. Jesus, I can't have lost her. I don't know what I'd do."

"Yeah. You'll miss all that money." And so would I.

"No, no. It's not that. I'd agree to a complete separation of funds. She keeps her family money, and I'll live off my business. It's doing okay. I need her by me."

He was slobbering now. Almost pathetic. He pulled into the parking lot behind my place and shut off the engine. He handed the file folder back to me.

"I want you to have every piece of information I have on her. Everything. You need to find her. I think I may have fucked up once too often."

I half-smiled to myself. This sounded like it was going to be work. Good money paying work. Really easy work, too. "Okay, come on up and let me know everything you know."

Chapter Four

I was slowly gaining appreciation for computers, but they are pretty useless for writing reports. I can write by hand faster than I can type, and writing notes on a laptop while I'm on a stakeout kind of blows my cover. Unfortunately, professionalism requires my reports to be typed because I have the handwriting of a doctor.

But when it comes to looking for someone who doesn't want to be found, a computer and friendship with a local whiz takes days off a pursuit. It adds legitimacy to the search, also. And legitimacy is everything.

Ernie told me the story in more detail once we retired to the relative coolness of the office.

"She seemed a little distant at breakfast yesterday. But you know Betty. Not the most relaxed person in town. I left to install a new oven at that kebab shop down the road, and when I came home, she wasn't there."

I handed him a beer and sat across from him at my kitchen table, pen in hand, a pad of paper in front of me. "Did you talk during the day?"

"No. I sent her a text around lunch, but she didn't answer. It was unopened on her phone when I got home last night." He took a mouthful of beer and wiped his mouth. "I thought at first it was because I was late getting home, but when I found the phone, I knew she'd left before noon." He looked at the pad of paper. "You going to write any of this down?"

I scribbled 'noon' and 'text' and looked at him. "Any place you think she might be?"

He shook his head. "I tried the obvious places. Her father's house. The beach place. Her sister's. None of them knew where she was. I think I might have pissed off her father, but I don't care at this point. I need to find her and talk to her."

He placed his hand on the file. "Everything is

in here. Everything I know about her. I can't do this without you. I'll pay whatever."

I sipped my beer and thought for a minute. Delicate balance, pricing. Too little, and you're undervaluing yourself, and nobody respects you. Too much, and you price yourself out of business. But this was a special case, for a special friend. A special situation.

I reached across the table and slid the folder to my side. "Pro bono, for this one. You're a good friend; this is the least I can do for you."

"No, no. I need to pay you. You need to give this your highest priority."

I patted him on the back of his hand. "Okay. $500 a day. Mate's rates. I'll give it my highest priority. Absolute highest. Give me a couple of days. I know a kid who is a bloody genius on computers, and with him digging through databases and me pounding the pavement, we'll track her down in no time. Trust me."

His eyes welled up. Jesus. "Thanks, Mac. I really owe you."

"Yeah, yeah. You let me know if she contacts you, right? Now get out of here and let me work."

I walked him to the door and told him I'd keep in touch. I checked my watch. It was too late to pick up my car. Fuck.

I sat back at the table and flipped through the file. Standard stuff. Bank account details, tax file number, lists of friends and acquaintances. Ernie had done a lot of the leg work for me. I closed my eyes and tried to remember the name. Cameron. Cameron Reese. Good kid. He got into a little trouble accessing data he shouldn't have a couple of years ago, but his youth got him off the hook. His youth and a little bit of help from me.

I found his mother's number in my phone and called.

"Lucy? Mac here."

"What's he done now?"

"Cameron? Nothing. I'm calling to hire him. I need him to help me track down someone."

"No illegal stuff." It wasn't a question.

"Absolutely not. All above board. I just need someone better at this damn machine than I am, and young Cam could use a break, right?"

She sighed. "You guarantee this doesn't get

him into trouble?"

"On my mother's eyes."

She grunted something that I assumed was consent and called for him to come to the phone. Background noise for a second. Then he picked up.

"Mr Durridge?"

"Mac. Call me Mac. I need to hire you for a couple of days. Three, max."

"What do you want me to do?"

"Help me find someone. Pop by tomorrow morning around 8:00, and I'll get you going, okay? A hundo a day."

"Really? That's not much."

"I'll double it if you're successful."

Cameron was a massive Type-A guy. He knocked at my door at 8:00 sharp, waking Lincoln and interrupting my morning newspaper. I pulled on a T-shirt and followed the mutt to the door. Cam stood a foot taller than me and had a lot more muscle than I did. Not your typical nerd. Or geek. Or whatever the hell they're called. Still was a little spotty, thought and sported a mere shadow of an attempted goatee.

"Good morning, Mac. Am I too early?"

"Just in time, kid. Coffee?"

He held up a can of energy drink. "I'm good. What is it you want me to do?"

"You know how you got into that frequent flyer site and added all those points to your card for the Bali trip?"

"That I didn't get to go on."

"Yeah, well, you got caught." I pointed to the chair behind my desk. "Sit."

"Mum said it wasn't something illegal."

I waggled my hand. "Not as illegal as last time."

Cam eased into the chair and tapped the spacebar. "Password?"

I gave him the credentials, making a mental note to change it when he was finished.

"So what is it you want me to do? Who am I supposed to find?"

I slid the folder to him and flipped it open. "You know Betty? She's missing. Ernie doesn't want the police involved because he thinks it's domestic and not foul play. I'm inclined to believe him. Dig around all the possible databases and see if you can find any recent activity."

"How recent?"

"Last twenty-four to thirty-six hours. I'm taking the pooch for a walk. Make yourself at home."

He put his head down and started in on the keyboard, furiously clicking away at something. I jangled the dog's lead, and he was at my feet instantly, sitting with an expectant look in his eyes and a big, happy dog smile.

When I returned, Cameron was trawling through a half dozen databases he'd accessed in ways I didn't want to know about. At first glance, it seemed like Betty really didn't want to be found. As rich as she was, you'd think she would be accustomed to the finer things in life, and finer things are generally acquired with plastic, not cash.

"Getting close, Cameron?"

He answered without looking away from the screen. "I've been in half a dozen places. She's not there. Not by that name, anyway."

"I'm getting some food. Keep looking at other places where you might think she is. I'll be back in a couple of hours."

"Staying in this one for a while. Checking for anyone who only used the store up here for the past month or so." Cameron pulled his eyes away from the screen. "Maybe she planned this in advance. I'll text you if I find something."

"Great. Thanks, kid."

The sun had risen a bit over three hours ago and at 9:00 a.m. it was already 32 degrees and climbing. And I was a bit tired. And with Sophie gone, nobody to cook my breakfast, The Pelican was the place to be.

I bought two scrambled egg and bacon wraps, and two coffees, and went back outside.

Barry "Baz" Simonsen sat on the sidewalk outside The Pelican, in frayed shorts, a formerly white T-shirt now a uniform grey and thongs that looked vintage. A very old Central Coast Mariners cap sat on his head. It looked like it had been weeks since he cleaned himself up. He sat with his back to the patio railing, his knees up and his arms resting on them.

I sat down beside him and handed him a wrap and a coffee.

He looked over at me, gave me a really slight

nod, and took them. He peeled the paper off the wrap and took a big bite. "What ya want?"

"You're turning into a cynic, Baz. Just wanted to say hi. How's it going?"

The sun skipped across the water, through the boats bobbing at their moorings and reflecting off the concrete in front of him. He squinted and pulled the brim of his hat lower, shading his eyes.

He took a sip of coffee and continued to ignore me.

I saw Jessie's car roll into the lot. It wasn't looking as pristine as it did yesterday. There was a plastic bag taped over the back passenger's side window. She detoured her walk into The Pelican to pass by us. She looked at us, frowned, and then aimed her scorn at Baz. "Hey, mate. Go home. Can't have you loitering out here."

"He's homeless. By definition, he doesn't have a home." I nodded toward her car. "How'd you break the window? Put the board through it?"

"Not really any of your business. Baz, get out of here."

Baz looked up at her with a smile on his face,

squinting at her silhouette. She flicked her ponytail and walked toward The Pelican's front door.

"Don't make me send my dad out. Mac, move him long, will you?"

I nudged Baz with my elbow. "Let's get around to the patio, Baz. It's too nice to go inside." We picked up our food and drink and moved around to the back. "You been keeping clean?"

He smiled at me, a piece of bacon on his teeth. "As a whistle." He nodded his head back and forth, equivocating. "Except for some Jack and Coke every so often."

A couple of uniformed constables came into The Pelican for breakfast, sitting on the patio. We slid a bit further around the corner from the dining area to stay out of their sight. I recognised the cops. They had picked Baz up a couple of times for public intoxication and weren't particularly sympathetic to his homeless plight. The one that looked like a rugby player gone to middle-aged fat was Carter, and the whippet was Ford. The skinny one tended to take the most delight in harassing Baz.

Jessie took their order and left for the kitchen

and Baz had closed his eyes to get a bit more recuperative rest when Ford cleared his throat. His first words caught my attention.

"Fuckin' Jackson."

I cocked an ear.

Carter replied. "Even off the force he's got us working all night."

I slid a bit to the right and got an eye on them.

Ford tore a thin strip from the paper napkin and slowly rolled it into a ball. "What do you figure happened?"

"Fuck knows. He's pissed off enough people in his life. Could have been his ex, or one of the many he's railroaded during his career."

Jessie came out to their table with two cups of coffee.

Ford smiled up at her. "Thanks, Jess." He took a sip and addressed his partner. "Had to be someone big to kill Jackson."

Fuck. Dead? I looked at Baz. He was devoted to the bacon and egg wrap and wasn't paying attention. I looked back at Ford and Carter. And Jessie, mouth agape.

Charter shook his head. "I don't know. He's let himself go the last coupla months." He looked at Jess, who had stopped her return to the kitchen and was staring at them. "You okay?"

"Jackson is dead?"

"Yeah, sorry. Didn't realise he was a friend of yours."

"Oh, Jesus, no. Not a friend." A smile split her face. "He's really dead? Holy fuck."

Carter looked at Ford, and they both looked at Jessie.

Ford cleared his throat. "You don't seem that upset, Jess. What's going on?"

"How'd he die? Was it slow and painful?"

I knew I liked Jessie. I would hate to be on her bad side. I sat back and watched and listened.

"Whoa. This guy was a former police officer. A little respect for the dead."

"Really, Carter? He killed Jimmy. I know he did. How he got the fuck out of jail is beyond me. I'm glad he's dead. He deserves no less. I'm only sorry I didn't do it myself." She smiled at both of them. "You've made my day, gentlemen. Breakfast will be out in a minute. And it's on the house."

Her ponytail snapped as she turned, a spring in her step as she returned indoors.

"Well, that was interesting. You hear anything about him killing Jimmy?"

Carter shook his head, frowning. "Huh. Jimmy was found not far from where Jackson currently lies, face down in the sand. Same beach. Kinda similar method."

"Jimmy was beaten to a pulp. Jackson didn't look like he was bruised up. I was at the scene when Jimmy was found. Completely different."

Carter shrugged. "Whatever. I'd heard rumours about Jackson and Jimmy, but nothing ever substantiated."

Jess walked out with a tray with two breakfast plates and a large pot of coffee. "Come by with good news like that again, and you'll always eat free. You didn't tell me what happened."

I needed to hear this.

"We really don't know. We were traffic at the scene. An early morning jogger found him at Budgie, in the dunes."

She slowly placed the tray on a table beside them and handed them their plates of food. "Near where Jimmy was found?"

Ford nodded. "Not that far away. I wouldn't make anything of it. It's a dark piece of road leading up to it. Handy place for a body dump."

She nodded and tucked the tray under her arm. "Poetic that Jackson's life ended where he ended someone else's." She thought for a second, then nodded, the smile returning to her face. "And good fucking riddance to him." She walked back to the interior of The Pelican with a bounce in her step.

Carter grunted. "That was strange."

Ford dipped toast in egg yolk. "Isn't all life strange? Hey, you hear what happened to the Rabbitohs?"

I tuned out. I'm not a big fan of League, and even if I were, I certainly wouldn't be barracking for the Rabbitohs. I slid back around the corner into the shade. Upwind of Baz, fortunately. The wrap was gone, and he was draining the coffee dregs.

"You hear that, mate? Jackson is dead."

He nodded. "Yeah. I know." He tipped back the cup and let the last drop of coffee land on his tongue. "Lily headed out to the beach about an hour ago. 'Parently Jackson was killed about the same place Jimmy was found. Dead as a doorknob."

I peeled the paper back from my now cold wrap. "How is it you always find out shit before me?"

He tapped the side of his nose. "Kidneys, mate." He belched. "Now, if you'll excuse me, it's time for my morning nap." He crossed his arms, and dropped his head onto his chest. Asleep in seconds. The life of one with not a care in the world.

I, on the other hand, had a date with a dead man.

Chapter Five

I walked across the street to my car and stopped in front of the empty spot. "Shit." It was still at Sal's.

I ran up the stairs and into my office. The kid was deep into something, fingers dancing across the keyboard.

He looked up as I entered. "Haven't found anything yet. Still looking, though." His attention turned back to the monitor almost instantly, dismissing me and my sweaty neck.

"You got a car, Cameron?"

He didn't look up. "My mum's. Why?"

I saw the keys on the desk. "The Honda?"

He stopped typing. "Is it okay? Nobody ran into it, did they? Mum'll never let me take it again."

I scooped the keys off the desk. "Not yet. But it *is* poking out a bit. I'll move it for you."

I parked Cameron's mum's car beside two marked police cars and an obviously unmarked car. There was nothing going on that I could see, so I walked up over the wooden boardwalk.

A couple of uniforms stood guard at a taped-off area, and Detective Sergeant Lily King, in a smart pantsuit, was slowly walking around Jackson who was face down in the sand.

I didn't know who the uniforms were, but I knew Lily well. "Hey, King. What killed him?"

She looked up and nodded me over. "Let him through, guys."

One of the uniforms lifted the tape.

Jackson's body had that settled look like someone in a deep sleep, muscles completely relaxed. It looked like him from the back. Slack fat, greasy singlet and those god-awful cargo shorts. "It *is*, Jackson, right?"

"It was. But no more. Just a meat sack now." She flipped her book closed and slid it into her back pocket. "Help me flip him over."

"You have a spare set of gloves?"

She tossed me a pair of latex gloves and squatted by his feet. "Grab his left shoulder and roll him."

I tucked Jackson's right arm alongside his body and nodded. We rolled the slack body onto its back. "Jesus, he's an ugly fuck."

"Why are you here?"

I shrugged. "Personal interest. We never got along at the best of times. Recently, even worse."

"The bank thing, right?"

"I didn't give much of a shit about the robbery. More than a bit pissed off that he walked for killing Jimmy and those two surfer dudes."

"You know how it goes. Either he cut a deal, or there wasn't enough to convict, or some other such bullshit. I'll be honest, I wasn't upset to see him leave the force. He was a poisonous influence on the younger squad members." She hooked her thumbs in her belt. "You get to keep any of the money? Rumour has it some's still missing."

"Not likely." I resisted the urge to squat down beside Jackson's corpse with King. "So what killed him?"

"Coroner will say for sure, but by my eyes, it looked like he was whacked on the head with a heavy blunt object. Could have showed you the contusion before we flipped him." She pointed at his fat flabby neck. "Red marks indicate he was then strangled."

"When?"

"I'll know for sure when I get the autopsy results, but I'm guessing between ten and midnight.

I looked around. "Pretty dark here at night. No streetlights. No moon. No witnesses, I take it?"

"Just the jogger who found him this morning. Put him off his day."

"I would imagine. Evidence?"

She held up a bag with a length of rubberised rope, about as big around as my pinkie finger and two metres long. "He was strangled with this, I think. Might be able to get some epithelial cells from it. I'll know later. Not much more than that. Dry, loose sand, so no footprints. Difficult to tell if there was a struggle, frankly."

I scratched the back of my head. "Had to be someone pretty big to subdue him. He was in pretty shit shape, but still not a lightweight." I nodded. "A big guy. Or two."

"Not necessarily. A blow to the back of the head could have knocked him out. Strangling an unconscious guy isn't that difficult."

I thought about that for a minute. "Tons of people with motives."

"Including you. Do you have an alibi for last night?"

"After ten? Asleep. No witnesses."

"You and Sophie split?"

"Oh, hell no. She's up in Newcastle for a couple of weeks. Or longer. Just me and Lincoln."

"He can't vouch for you?"

"He's a Border Collie."

"Ah." She flipped open her notebook. "When's the last time you saw Jackson?"

"Yesterday afternoon. You're not really including me in your 'person of interest' list, are you?"

"Covering all bases, Mac. Where was it, and

what did you talk about?"

I pointed down the parking lot side of the dune. "At the burger place, and I bumped into him with Jessie."

"From the Pelican?" She scribbled something in her book.

"Yeah."

"She was with Jackson?" She raised an eyebrow. "Seems unlikely."

"She was with me. Linc and I met her on the beach and were walking her back to her car when we bumped into Jackson. Coincidentally."

"How did that go?"

Not well. Risky telling her that, though. "Well, we don't like each other. There were no hugs shared. Grange was there, too, feeding him a burger. Maybe ask him. He'll be a bit more dispassionate about the encounter." I paused. "Frankly, I wanted to slug Jackson when I saw him, but I restrained myself. Honest." Mostly.

"Maybe you came back here with him last night and let loose that restraint."

"Not my style. If I had killed him, there would

have been a significant amount of bruising around his face and blood everywhere."

King looked like she was suppressing a smile. She wrote something in her little notebook, flipped it closed and slid it into her back pocket. "Thanks, Mac. Appreciate the conversation."

I moved to one side as a couple of guys walked under the tape with a stretcher and bag. Trash collection.

King watched them manoeuvre Jackson's body into a body bag.

My phone vibrated in my pocket. "No problem, Lil. If you need anything else, let me know." I held up my phone. "Gotta take this."

I turned my back on her and walked back down the boardwalk to the parking lot. Stuck my earbuds in and answered the call. "Mac Durridge Investigations. Mac speaking. What can I do for you?"

"This is Malcolm Durridge? The PI up on the coast?" The voice was male, young and vaguely, annoyingly familiar.

"I prefer Mac. Who is this?"

"You don't recognise the voice? I'm

offended."

"And I'm really fucking busy. Don't have time for guessing. Talk to you later."

"No, wait. I'm Steve Ryan."

He stopped after that like I should know who he was. I let the silence build for a bit.

"Yeah, so?"

"Home and Away? The lifeguard for three seasons a few years ago?"

Nothing. I watched very little television, and what little I did didn't include Home and Away. "Not a clue, mate. Sorry. Is that it?"

"I talked to your partner, and he said you'd be happy to help."

"Partner?"

"Cameron, I think his name was."

Fuck. "Not a partner. And help you with what?"

"I've just been cast in a gritting drama where I play a hard-boiled PI, and I think I need to do a bit of research."

"Gritting?" Jesus Christ. "You mean 'gritty', right? And no way. I'm not going to be a babysitter and this isn't a stupid movie. Go look somewhere else."

"Look, I'm from there. Haven't been back in yonks. People say you're the man. It would mean a tonne to me."

"Blow it out your arse, kid." I hung up and blocked his number. He sounded like a persistent fuck. And like a pain in the ass I didn't need right now.

Chapter Six

King was walking back down to her car. I trotted after her. Through loose sand. Damn near killed me.

"Hey, King, you finished? That's it?"

She looked back up the hill toward the spot where Jackson was found. "Yeah." She turned back to her car. "Not much more evidence to collect here. Pretty straightforward."

I let her walk away to her car. The marked cars left the parking lot first, one turning left and the other right. They were off to catch speeders or drivers who let their registration lapse or maybe join a roadside breath test set up.

A minute later, King rolled out and turned left, back toward the station.

I walked back up to the crime scene. She wasn't wrong. If the tape weren't up, you wouldn't know that something happened. No blood. They'd taken the length of leg cord. There were no viable footprints in the sand. And it's unlikely there would have been any witnesses after ten last night.

I stood on a slight rise above the depression that had recently held Jackson. It was only metres away from where Jimmy was found, beat to within an inch of his life, almost five months ago. Jackson had paid a couple of thugs to lure him out to the beach and beat him to death.

I don't blame Jessie for being furious about Jackson's release. I had him dead to rights. He tried framing me for a bank heist and then for Jimmy's murder, but I dug up enough evidence, or so I thought, to put him away for a long, long time.

And now he was dead.

I'm not that fond of coincidences.

But it was appropriate, I guess. And he had a shit-ton of enemies. King would have a ballroom full of suspects, many of whom were her colleagues.

I turned around and looked back up the beach. It was too hot. Flat out too hot. And you'd think the beach would be packed in this heat, but it was too hot for even that. The sand burned through the soles of my shoes, and the onshore breeze was negligible.

Fuck this. Thank god I didn't *have* to be out here.

I made my way through the burning sand to Cameron's mum's car. Had to sit sideways in the front seat while the car warmed up and the air conditioning cooled down. I could barely touch the steering wheel.

After a couple of minutes, when the air coming out of the vents was slightly below the temperature of the sun, I closed the door and started back to the office—emphasis on started.

Not even ten metres out of the parking lot, after my left turn, my phone rang. The display showed me that it was Jessie, and after a second's hesitation, I answered it.

"What's going on, Jess?"

"Do you watch 'Home and Away', Mac?"

Oh, Jesus. "Never have. And do not tell me

that—"

"Do you know Steve Ryan? The Actor?" She said it with a capital A. You could tell by the way she said it. "He just left here, and he's looking for you."

I pulled over. "Where is 'here'?"

"The Pelican. He said he had already been talking to you? Said that he was going to work with you on some cases or some such stuff? Are you going to be back here today? Can you bring him over here for lunch?"

"Goodbye, Jess. Glad you're feeling better." I thumbed off the phone and dropped it on the seat beside me. And now I'd have to dodge a Steve Ryan until he got tired of hanging around.

It was a short drive to the office, and when I parked behind the building, the last thing I wanted to do was get out of the car.

I turned off the engine, stepped into the heat, and headed up the stairs to the office, drenched in sweat by the time I got to the top.

And when I opened the door, the chilled good looks of who I assumed to be Steve fucking Ryan was the first thing I saw.

Chapter Seven

I'm pretty sure there isn't a life form on Earth I despise more than an actor. All make-believe, fake faces, plugged hair and not a genuine bone in their body. I pointed at the door. "Out."

Ryan crossed his arms. His muscled, tanned arms. He stood about six feet in the old numbers, very fit and dressed in formal casual. A Polo shirt tucked into a pair of skinny jeans, with tasselled deck shoes on his feet. The buckle on his belt was big enough to serve nachos.

He smiled. But his eyes frowned. Probably not accustomed to getting told what to do. "Mac, Mac. You haven't heard what I want yet."

"You've got a part; you want to roll with me. Except I work alone and have absolutely *no* desire to babysit a spoiled, useless man-child." He flexed a bicep, probably reflexively, but it sure looked like a threat. "Please, get out." I stepped to one side to give him room and a not so subtle hint.

He didn't move. Looked around the office, taking in the furnishings. "A grand a day. No, two grand."

"A day?"

"Each day I'm here, with you, seeing what it is you do. Two week's worth, maybe?"

Well, money talks, right? Quick math, I'm looking at twenty grand, or more, just for putting up with the teeth. Fuck, they were white. I stuck out my hand. "Deal. We start now. What is it you want to know?"

"Really, Mac—can I call you Mac? I need to know what the banality of life is for a PI. I suspect there's a lot of drinking coffee and eating donuts in an all-night stakeout, but I'm willing to learn."

"Been months since an all-nighter. Just looking for a missing person right now." I nodded in

Cameron's direction. "And he's doing most of the work. Hope you like coffee. There's a lot of it in your future, usually at The Pelican, shooting the shit."

"That's the place where the lovely Jess works."

I levelled a finger at him. "Hey, she's only—"

I was interrupted by a sharp knock and King poking her head in the door. "Mac? Need to talk to you." She spotted Ryan and stepped into my office. "Mac, you didn't say you knew Steve Ryan." She didn't take her eyes off him. She walked towards him slowly, like she was easing up to a spooked horse. "What brings you back, Stevie? Do you remember me?"

He cocked his head. "Lily? Wow. It's been what, fifteen years?" He looked at me. "Lily used to babysit me. Geeze, it's been a long time. A different life, right?" He hugged her, and her face turned the colour of ten hours in the summer sun.

"Oh, my goodness."

Right. What a load of shit. "You came in here looking for me, King. What's up?"

She took one long, lingering look at Steve, cleared her throat and returned to me. "Need you to come into the station for some questions."

"Me? Why?"

"It looks like you're one of the last people to see the victim before he was killed. Come downtown with me?"

Steve chuckled. "Downtown? This place doesn't have a downtown. Hey, can I come with? Will be good background."

I opened my mouth to object and remembered the money. "Lily, if it's okay with you, let him come along, okay?"

She didn't need much convincing. "As long as he doesn't interfere with the investigation."

Really? "I'm part of an investigation?"

"Just questions to clarify timelines and what not."

"Yeah, I'm coming along." Steve slapped me on my back, almost driving me to the floor. "Let's go, Mac. You wanna come with me or with Lily? I bet she's not driving a convertible."

I bet she wasn't. I dropped Cameron's keys on the desk. "Text me if you find anything."

The three of us single-filed down the stairs. Lily's unmarked Holden was sitting in the parking lot behind the building. Beside a cherry red Porsche 911 something or other. "I'll be with Steve, Lily." I slid down into the front seat. "You know where you're going, right kid?"

He half-grinned. "Been there a couple of times in my youth. Pretty sure I can find my way."

No interrogation room this time. King dragged a chair from one of the other desks, and it was a cosy threesome with King on her side of the desk and Steve and I scrunched together on the other side.

She fussed with some papers on her desk, filed a couple of folders and then picked up a pen and pad of paper. "I need more details about when you saw Jackson yesterday."

Steve interrupted before I could form a sentence. "Who's Jackson? Wait, fat fuck Tommy? He's the victim? What happened?"

King looked at me, narrowed her eyes, and I'm pretty sure she started thinking of ways to fuck me over. "Mac?"

"He's actually got a point. What happened? What have the MEs found out?"

"Hit on the head, hard, with a blunt object. Like I said. It cracked his skull and most likely rendered him unconscious. Then, that length of cord was used to strangle him. There's a bruise on the back of his neck, probably from a knee, and his trachea was completely crushed." She tapped her fingers on her desk. "Mac? Tell me about the time on the beach yesterday."

I dry scrubbed my face and thought. I didn't think I could add anything to her investigation, but I'd been on her side of the desk before. Something I would think was completely innocuous could be the piece to the puzzle that showed her the complete picture.

But something was off. "No task force? Jackson was a cop. I'd expect a war room with a whiteboard and old coffee and a bustling hive of activity."

She shrugged. "He wasn't well loved. And no longer a cop when he was killed. Tell me about yesterday afternoon."

"I was walking Lincoln on the beach—that same one. I ran into Jessie surf-kiting or kite-surfing or whatever it's called and helped her carry her stuff back to her car. When we came down the path to the parking lot she saw Jackson and had a run at him."

"What was Jackson doing there?"

"No clue. He was there with Grange."

"Grange?"

"Exactly. We pulled them apart and Jessie spouted venom at him."

"Any idea why?"

I scratched my jaw. "She thought he was behind bars, serving time for killing Jimmy. The kid from the bank," I added unnecessarily—she was nodding as soon as I said his name.

"Another reason why there's no task force. A good sized contingent of the force thinks the world's a better place without him." She wrote something on the pad. "What happened after that? Who left first?"

"Jessie. I had a chat with Jackson after she left. He's a dick. Was a dick. He'd put on a few pounds, and his hair went grey really fast. Started looking like that arsehole DA from the 'Making a Murderer' doco. Who do you think is good for this?"

"Early days, Mac." She looked at her watch. "And I've got more to do." She looked at Steve.

"Thanks for not butting in all the time."

Steve nodded and stood, a sombre cast to his face. "Nice seeing you again, Lily. We should catch up sometime."

Her face almost split in half. "Oh, that would be excellent. You're staying with Mac?"

Hell no. "Not a chance."

"No, no. I wouldn't think of imposing. Ask for me at The Pelican. I'll use that as my focal point. But I will be hanging with Mac during waking hours. Preparing for a role."

"Let's get going, Steve-o. I've got to get my car."

"We can use mine while I'm here."

"Wouldn't think of it." We stepped out of the station and into the heat. "I'm lousy at giving directions. Do you know where Sally's auto shop is?"

Steve shook his head. "Never heard of it."

We got into his car. I ran my fingers along the stitching on the dash. Nice, supple leather. "Hank's place. Ring a bell?"

Steve pulled his sunglasses off of his ridiculously thick hair and put them on, backed out and headed north. "I know it well."

He had lost the cheeky, on-top-of-the-world attitude that he'd exhibited when he showed up. I didn't feel like punching him in the neck any more. "You okay? Seem like a different person."

He didn't answer for a minute. He seemed to be thinking about what to say. "I knew Tom. I didn't know him well, but I knew enough to steer clear of him. He had a habit of brutalising younger kids."

"He must have been ten years older than you."

"Nine. Imagine a sixteen-year-old putting the boots to a seven-year-old. And he enjoyed it."

"Fuck." We rode in silence for a bit. "So why aren't you more pleased that he's been removed from the face of the Earth?"

"I am. But I've never felt joy at someone's death before. It disturbs me. Not in harmony with the universe right now."

"Hey, it's okay to be happy that a fuck-knuckle is removed from the dance card. He wasn't a nice person."

He shrugged. "Nonetheless. Why'd you get Hank's place to fix your car? Even as a kid, I knew they were on the shady side of things."

"Shady? I think you're looking for 'gang affiliated', right? They are. They also do a good job and know better than to rip me off." I looked at the clock on his dash. "Step on it, will you? They close in thirty."

Chapter Eight

Cops need to work on making their unmarked cars a lot less obvious. They are always sedans, always plain, with a couple of extra antennas. They may as well be painted. One was parked outside Sal's place when we arrived, and it looked familiar.

I could hear him from outside.

"Well, I should let you go. My best to Sally."

Then there was the metallic slam of a bonnet closing, and I could hear Dick say, "Tell her yourself. Where the fuck is Durridge? If he's not here in the next five I'm closing up."

I walked into the garage, past the 'no customers beyond this point' sign and nodded at Dick. "Got here just in time." I held my hand out for the keys. "What do I owe you?" I looked over at Grange. "Hey, Grange. You getting your car fixed here, too? That's hilarious."

Grange ignored me, and Dick pulled a cloth from his back pocket and wiped his hands, walking slowly toward me. "It's going to cost you. Took a lot of work. And it's an old as fuck piece of shit. Hard to find parts."

"It was just the plugs, right?"

He shook his head. "New distributor cap and points, too. All up, including my labour, $425."

He was less than a metre from me, occupying a lot of space. I fought the urge to take a backward step. So I leaned in a bit. "You're fucking kidding. $100, you said."

"I said nothing of the sort, Mac. Maybe Sal did, but she ain't here right now." He held out his hand. "$425 or you don't get the keys back."

Grange was watching this with a funny smile, arms crossed, still looking like he just put on his suit. The bastard never seemed to break a sweat. But I was starting to feel it. $425 was a bit rich. A couple more hundred and the dealer could have done it.

Steve nudged me to one side and pulled out his wallet. "You take plastic, right? And he's going to want a receipt." He pushed a credit card into Dicks hand. "And we're in a bit of a hurry."

Dick looked at Grange, then down at the card in his hand. "3% service charge for plastic."

"Whatever. Speed it up."

I snatched the card out of Dick's hand and gave it back to Steve. "Obliged, mate, but you're paying me enough already."

I took my wallet out and counted out $400. "Discount for cash, Dick. Take it or leave it."

Steve did one of his flex things and crossed his arms. Dick smiled and shook his head. He took the money and butted the edges neatly together. "I'll let Sal know you still owe her $25." He backed up a couple of steps and underhanded the keys to me. "Get the fuck out. I'm closing up."

I hopped in the old piece of shit car, slid the key in the ignition, held my breath a second, and twisted. It coughed once and started, purring like it hadn't in years. The guy was an arsehole, but he knew his cars.

Steve leaned into the driver's window. "I'll follow you back in case the fix isn't permanent." He winked and looked back at Dick, who was ignoring him.

Grange put his hand on Steve's shoulder and stood him upright. "You all need to leave now. The man is closing up shop."

I saluted him with two fingers and put the car in reverse and started backing out. Halfway out of the garage, my phone started vibrating in my pocket. Dick was walking me out, less than a meter in front of the car, following me as I backed out onto the street. I didn't want to stop and dig my phone out. It could go to voicemail this time.

That turned out to be a bad decision.

I slowed a bit as I crossed the threshold with the back wheels, and Dick slapped on the hood. "Hurry it up, you fuck."

It would be so easy to pop it in drive and run his ass over. Grange was there, but I'm sure he would see it as justifiable homicide. I took a deep, soothing breath and visualised Dick splattered all over the garage floor, then increased the speed out of Sal's garage.

I pulled over by the side of the road, and while Steve was getting his car and pulling in behind me, I checked my phone.

It was a call from Sophie. No voicemail, which wasn't a surprise. Not many people use it any more. I was surprised to learn from Cameron that most kids didn't even use email any more. Instant messaging and SnapChat, whatever the fuck that is, had replaced it.

I scrolled through the call menu and rang Sophie back. It went immediately to voicemail. No rings. The phone was dead. Maybe it died while she was calling me, and that's why she didn't leave even a short voice message. I didn't leave a message, because, really, who does that anymore?

Steve pulled in behind me, and just as I was about to put my car in gear and head home, his door opened, and he got out of the car.

He hopped in the passenger seat and finger-combed his hair back out of his eyes. "Is it just me, or is Grange a psycho?"

"You know him?"

Steve shook his head. "Never saw him before. Must be new since I left, because I got to meet a lot of the cops when I was younger."

"You know his name?"

"You said hi to him. He's got that greasy look that reminds me of silverfish." He pulled a face. "I wouldn't trust him to tell me the weather. Keep an eye out for him."

"I thought you were learning from me. Get back to your car. I've got to get back and send Cameron home before he bankrupts me."

The car ran well all the way back. Steve stayed close to my tail. Say what you want about Sal's crew, but they were good under the hood. I pulled into my parking spot, and Steve and his convertible parked beside me.

I leaned against my car and watched Steve put the roof up on his car. Not like the old days, when you had to yank it forward from some hiding place in the back, forcing the offset clips closed to keep it tight. A lid opened at the back of the car, just behind the back seats, and a metal roof unfolded and slowly settled into place. Steve needed minimal effort to clip it into place before he hopped out.

He clapped me on the shoulder and placed a

thick ream of banknotes in my hand. "Today was worth it. I'll be staying across the street at The Pelican. I'm pretty sure they'll have a room. I'll give you a call in the morning. Cool?"

I folded the money and wedged it into my jeans pocket. "Cool." Extremely cool. I'd milk this for all I could. This was good money.

I watched him cross the street, then ran up the stairs two at a time. It wasn't as hot now. The sun was on the horizon, and the heat had leached from the air.

The air-conditioning was still blasting when I went in; it was too cold for comfort. Cameron had his head down, banging furiously away at the keyboard. I turned off the air conditioning unit and sat on the edge of the desk. "Any luck?"

He shook his head. "I'm starting to think she might be dead."

"She's well and truly gone to ground." I peeled two hundred off the pile of notes Steve had given me. "You're doing great. Head home now. It's been a long day. Come back tomorrow around noon, okay?"

Cameron looked at the money in his hands, folded it in half and jammed it in his wallet. "Sure thing,

Mac. See you tomorrow."

He was out the door and down the steps in seconds. I looked at the computer screen. Didn't understand a thing on it.

I took out my phone and called Sophie again. Still straight to voicemail. I sent her a text message that she'd get when she finally got around to charging it. *Miss you. Love you. Don't be gone too long. I can't cook.*

I looked at my phone for a second, hoping for a response.

None.

I sent a second message to a different number. *You're doing good, Betty. Nobody has the slightest clue where you are. Keep your head down a few more days. Ernie is getting frantic. :)*

I just learned the smiley-face thing.

Chapter Nine

My sleep was interrupted by the dulcet marimba tones produced by my phone. It must have been going on for a long time before it registered. I had nine missed calls. Ten, now. I squinted at the number, trying to remember where I'd seen it before when it started up again. Persistent arsehole.

"Who are you and what's so fucking important?" I swung my feet to the floor.

"Mac, Steve here. I'm not in your phone yet?"

"You called me ten times?" I stood and stretched and considered the trade-off between a lot of money every day against the persistent annoyance of this fucking prat. "Wait. I blocked your number yesterday."

"I got a new number. I'm just making sure you're not trying to duck me."

I took the phone from my head and looked at the time. Jesus. "It's seven in the morning, and you're afraid I'm ducking you? What time do you normally wake up?"

"Up since five. Pilates and a bit of iron work, and a run before breakfast. And now I'm starving. Let's get together for breakfast. I'm buying."

I'm definitely taking advantage of this. "The Pelican. Twenty minutes."

Steve was leaning against the wall, charming the panties off Jessie. I walked up behind him and popped the back of his knee in that time-honoured trick to make someone look foolish by almost falling over. He didn't even budge.

He looked over his shoulder and smiled. "Mac. Just having a chat with Jessie about you. You broke her heart, Mac. Not cool, pretty lady like this."

She blushed and play-slapped him on the shoulder with a menu. "Stop it Steve."

"Yeah, stop it, Steve." I pushed past him and sat at a booth. "Can I get a large long black and a menu, Jess?"

It's sad to see a beautiful face like hers scowl. She flashed a quick smile at Steve and dropped the menu on the table. Steve sat across from me.

He leaned forward, resting his elbows on the table. "You're a bit of a dick, aren't you?"

"So what do you expect to get from this arrangement between us? I know what I'll be getting."

"The money's nothing." He pulled his sunglasses off of the top of his head and tucked one arm into the front of his shirt. "I was passed over for a couple of the Underbelly roles because—well, I don't really know why. It's probably because I've been typecast in light and fluffy pieces, like that lifeguard gig. And another time, I was a recurring real estate agent. Anyway, I just landed a part as a private eye. I want to nail this. *Need* to nail this. I want to get out of the pretty-boy rut." He picked up the menu. "I'm hoping you can help with that." He flipped through the pages. "Anything healthy in this?"

"Okay, first thing you've got to realise is that

the life of a PI is not a healthy life." I nodded at the tight T-shirt and bulging biceps. "None of us look like you. We're fairly soft around the middle and feed on greasy foods, usually while sitting in a car waiting for something to happen. Forget the healthy food." I waved Jessie over. I was starved, and my benefactor was going to pay.

"Still. I need to stay in shape for other roles." He closed his menu and handed it to Jessie. "I'll have a large fruit salad with yoghurt and a cup of green tea."

I smiled and handed my menu to Jess. "Big breakfast, forget the grilled tomato and add a couple of extra rashers, okay? And keep the cup full."

She scribbled on an order pad and walked back to the kitchen, glancing over her shoulder at Steve several times on the way.

I tapped on the table to get Steve's attention. "She's nineteen, mate. A little young for you."

He shrugged. "Legal, though. And very fit."

"Don't be an arsehole. Look, I don't have that much going on right now. Tracking down Betty is about it. Business has its ups and downs, and right now, it's in the downs." I placed my palms down on the table and leaned forward a bit. "So, like I said, I don't know what you'll get out of this arrangement. But if you're happy, I'm happy. A couple grand a day happy."

"Who's Betty again?"

"Wife of a friend. Disappeared about a couple of days ago. No cops, yet, because husband thinks it's just an angry spat."

"So she just got tired of the guy."

"Possible. You can help by loosening tongues as we drive around asking questions."

"No problem. So, for now, we can chat. I'll buy the breakfast, you can tell me war stories."

Jessie arrived with a large bowl of fruit and a tea service for Steve. "I'll be out with yours in a minute, Mac."

I nodded. Friendly service for a change. I was lit by the shine from Steve-o's glow. Lucky me. "My war stories are pretty boring."

"You were front and centre in that bank thing a few months ago, though. Right?"

I hate the Internet. "Yeah, not much there. A couple of idiots tried to rob the bank from the inside, and when the head office called a surprise audit, they panicked. Morons, really. Jackson was one of them."

"And he walked."

I shook my head. "You got me on that one. I don't know the details. Must have ratted out Harris."

"Who's that?"

"The bank manager. Was. In Silverwater for no less than ten years, I hear. If he lasts that long."

"And now Jackson's dead. Makes you think." Steve stuffed a couple of pieces of watermelon in his mouth. "Right?"

Jess placed my plate of food in front of me and topped up my coffee. Very friendly today. "It is an interesting point, but your babysitter seems to have it well in hand."

He frowned in thought for a second, then smiled. "Lily. Right. Yeah, is she a good cop?"

"One of the best, I think. Now shut up and let me eat this before it becomes a plate of congealed grease."

Steve sat back in his chair, watching me devour more calories than any man needs in a day. It was a bit of a patronising condescension he showed me, but I'd let him. For a week or so. No problem.

I wiped up the last bit of egg yolk with my last bit of toasted Turkish. It takes planning to do that, and I was becoming an expert. "One more thing to do, and we'll check on Cam's progress with his electronic Betty hunt. You're paying, right?"

Steve nodded.

"Good stuff. Add two large take-away long blacks and a couple of bear claws to go. I've got to hit the head."

"I don't drink coffee."

"Don't care. Neither one is for you."

I did what I had to do in the men's room, wiping my hands on my pants because, again, there were no paper towels in the lav. Steve met me at the door with the two coffees and bag of pastries. "What are these for?"

"Who are those for. Not what." I took the coffee and left him holding the bag. "Follow me."

Baz was in his normal spot, sitting with his back against the patio railing, watching people or cars or maybe just staring blankly into space. It was hard to tell some days. I sat on his left and pointed at Steve. "Pull up a seat. Say 'hi' to my friend, Barry. Baz will work."

"I won't fuckin' work. I don't needs to work. Who is this guy? He looks kinda familiar."

Steve slowly settled to the sidewalk, wrinkling his nose as he descended into the Baz stink zone. "Jesus Christ, man. You shit yourself?"

I handed Baz one of the coffees and the bag of pastries. "Take it easy, Steve. Baz has proven to be very helpful in the past."

Steve sat for a minute, then pushed himself up. "No way. I can't take the smell. I'll meet you back at your office, Mac. Sorry."

Baz watched him walk away, then looked into the bag. "More for me. Thanks, Mac." He took one out and sniffed. "Who's the himbo?"

I laughed. "Apparently, something big on the TV. From around here at one point, then got too big for the berg. Steve Ryan. You heard of him?"

"Nah." He chewed on the bear claw. "So, what's going on with you?"

"Nothing much. Tracking down Betty. Let me

know if you hear anything. Pretty dead other than escorting Steve-o around."

"I mean with the lady friend."

I looked at him. "What do you know?"

He sipped coffee and shrugged at the same time, dribbling through his stubble on to his dirty T-shirt. "She ain't been around for a week or so."

"Two days. She's up in Newcastle, visiting her sister."

He shook his head. "I just saw her sister. Youse two are on the outs, hey?"

I rubbed an eye with the heel of my hand. "You need to back off on the booze, mate. She's up at her sister's." I stood and clapped him on the shoulder. "I'll see you around. I've got an actor to babysit."

"Betcha that's paying good."

I grinned. "Fantastic."

I turned to leave and a marked police car and King, in her unmarked sedan, pulled to the front of The Pelican. King led the way in, and less than a minute later, she was leading Jessie out in handcuffs.

I ran out in front of her, blocking their progress and caught an ugly glare from her. "What's going on?"

I looked at Jessie. Her pale face was almost swallowed by her eyes, huge with disbelief. "Jess, what's happening?"

King gently pushed me to one side and marched Jess toward the marked car. "Don't make me pull you in for obstruction, Mac. This is a clean collar. Stay out of the way."

Chapter Ten

"What the fuck?" I watched King pull away, the marked car carrying a frightened Jessie following close behind.

Baz shuffled up beside me. "The plot thickens."

"Indeed it does, my friend. Indeed it does. What the hell is going on?"

A crowd had built around the front door, and I struggled to get through. Baz followed. By my reckoning, if he went first he would have parted the crowd like Moses did to the sea, just on smell. But he's not a leader, I guess.

Gerry, Jessie's father, was consoling Susie, his

wife. I held back. I had a nasty feeling that maybe something I had said to Lily had instigated this.

Gerry kissed the top of his wife's head and looked up. He saw me and caught my eye, motioning me over. "Mac, I've got to go to the station. Sue's in no shape to go, but I don't want to leave her alone. Can you stay with her?" He looked down into his wife's face. "That okay with you, Sue?"

She sniffed and took a step back. "Go. Get her out of there and back here, Gerry. Do it." She stood straighter and gently pushed him toward the door. "Go."

She waited for him to leave, then turned to face me. "Mac. What brings you here?"

"What did King say when she arrested Jess?"

Sue crossed her arms. "They say she killed Jackson. Ridiculous. Not that I'm sorry to see him gone, but there's no way that Jessie could have or would have."

"Was Jessie home the night before last, Sue?"

"I'm not talking about this right now. I need to get a barrister. I don't know anyone. All of our legal business is business stuff."

I dug my phone out of my pocket and scrolled through recent calls. "I got a guy."

"Of course you do."

Sue calmed down, and she and I headed to the police station, where we agreed to meet Alf, my trusted legal guy.

Alfred Dean worked the opposite of the aisle when I was on the force, defending anyone and everyone. I grew to both hate and admire him. He worked really hard for his clients. And some of his clients paid very well, although you'd never know it. He carried at least 20 kg more than he should, rarely spent more than $10 on a haircut, and most of his clothes should have been donated to a worthy charity months ago. His car, usually the number one lawyer's status symbol, barely beat mine in terms of classiness.

Sue got in the front of my car and slammed the door shut harder than she needed to. I winced. I was sympathetic to her feelings, but this thing needed to last me for a few more years. She was seething. And I didn't blame her. This was so many levels of bullshit. "There's no way she did this, Sue."

Her look at me would kill small mammals. "No fucking shit, Sherlock."

We lucked out and hit all three red lights on the way to the station. The air conditioning in the car wasn't keeping her cool. She pointed at a gap at the curb near the police station. "Park there."

"Yes, ma'am." Alf was standing on the front steps of the station, looking at his watch. "Alf. Over here."

He nodded toward the station, and I shook my head. "We'll talk a bit out here first, okay?"

Alf pulled the collar from his neck like a bad Dangerfield impression. "It's fucking hot out here, Mac. What's going on? You were kinda vague. You in trouble again?"

"Jessie's been picked up. She's going to be charged with Jackson's murder, by the sounds of it." I nodded at Sue. "You know Sue, right?"

Alf stuck out his hand. "The Pelican. Right. Wait, how in the hell is Jessie supposed to have killed someone twice her size?"

Sue's arms were crossed. Not subtle body language. "She didn't." She looked at me. "You sure about this guy?"

"I'm sure about this guy. Alf, can you get her out as fast as possible and find out what they have on her?"

"Absolutely. Who picked her up?"

"Lily King."

"Get out of the heat and I'll see what I can do."

I sat with Sue at a coffee shop beside the police station for over three hours. We did a lot of no talking. I had other things to do, but I couldn't leave her there. It's like we were stuck together with the trouble Jessie was in. I called Alf half a dozen times, and Sue called Gerry, and between us, we left half a dozen messages for them to hurry up.

I was dialling for what I thought was the seventh time when Gerry, Alf and Jess walked into the cafe. Chairs clattered as Sue surged to her feet and converged on them. I held back and let the hugs happen.

I mentioned Alf over, and we sat. "You turned your phone off?"

"I knew you'd be calling. Didn't need the

distraction. Trust me to do my job, okay?"

"So what's the deal?"

"Wait for the parents. They need to know, too."

"Gerry, too?"

"He wasn't present for most of the discussions. Jessie is a legal adult. They didn't need to let him in."

"Fuck." I looked over at Jessie and her parents. There was steel in their collective spines. Good. They'd need some fight in them. Gerry looked over the top of his wife's head at me and I motioned him over.

I waited until they were settled. "Okay, Alf. Talk."

He took a deep breath. "It doesn't look the greatest." He held up his hands and stopped the interruptions. "Hear me out. It doesn't. Jessie has been bailed. Gerry put The Pelican up for security. I attempted to convince the Judge that Jessie wasn't a flight risk, but the case against her is very strong. Honestly, I'm surprised she got bailed at all. They've got a very compelling case."

Jessie slapped both hands down on the table. "They can't have anything. I did *not* kill that arsehole.

Jesus."

Her mother placed a hand over one of Jessie's. "That temper isn't helping you any. Why Jessie, Alf?"

"Grange witnessed her going after Jackson at the beach. You were a witness, too, Mac. Grange's statement went three pages. It included his discussion with Jackson and your altercation, Jessie. He even mentioned your comment that you'd finish him the next time you saw him." He picked at a piece of paper napkin. "And that night, Jackson was killed. The blow to his head is consistent with a smash to the head with her sailboard."

Jessie slumped back in her seat. "And thousands of others."

"I know, Jessie. I made that point. Let me finish." He sighed. "The blow to the head didn't kill him. Knocked him out, if that. It might have only stunned him. Then someone, it's alleged that someone was Jessie, kneeled on Jackson's back and strangled him with the leg rope. Jessie has no alibi. She's certainly strong enough to do it. And she had motive." He wiped the corners of his mouth.

Sue visibly deflated. "She didn't do it."

"We know," I said. "None of us doubt that. Let Alf finish. How did you get her bailed?"

"I had a chat with the judge. We go back quite a long time. Jessie's young age, the fact that she wasn't a continued threat, that she had family here locked into a profitable business that they were willing to put up for collateral clinched it."

Jessie leaned forward. "Whoa, whoa. What do you mean, not a 'continued threat'? I was *never* a threat. I." She slapped her hand on the table. "Did." Slap "Not." Slap. "Kill him."

Susie put her arm around her daughter. "We know, Jessie." She looked at Alf. "So what's the defence?"

"I need to find out what the prosecution has. I'll know later today. Once I know, we'll reconvene and start picking apart their case."

"So why don't you find out who actually did it?"

"It's not as easy as that, Jess. My job is to defend you, not play detective." He looked at me. "I'm not the PI at the table anyway." He stood. "I'll head back and find out what I can find out, okay? Go home and I'll catch up with you there."

Baz leaned in close and whispered in my ear. "Mate, you've got to help her, right?"

Ah, shit. "I don't—"

Jess reached across the table and grabbed my arm. "Mac, I'm sorry I called you an arsehole. Find who killed Jackhole, just in case Alf can't pick enough holes. Please?" She looked at her parents. "We can pay him, right?"

I thought about Steve and his money and opened my big mouth. "Don't worry about it. We're friends. It's the least I can do." I'm getting soft in my old age. "Tell me everything you were doing the night of."

Alf interrupted. "I need to do some paperwork with Gerry and Sue. We'll be back at The Pelican."

"We'll stay here and talk," said Jessie. "I don't want anyone I know interrupting me."

It was a pretty vanilla story. No alibi, no witnesses to her doing nothing. And by her accounts, she did nothing. She had parked her car on a side street near the beach and sat on a dune at Jewfish Point, contemplating the unfairness of life. It was pitch black out there, the cooling breeze a nice counterpoint to the still hot sand. She told us she sat out there until almost midnight before she came home.

I asked to look at her hands and she held them out in front of me, palms down.

"No, the other way." I took them and gently turned them palms up. Her hands were red, a couple of small blisters at the junction of her fingers and palms. "What's this?"

She pulled them away and placed them on her lap. "From the kite surfing. It's been months. My hands are soft."

"When was your car broken in to?"

I watched realisation dawn on her face. "Oh, shit. It was that night. My kite bag was taken."

"You reported it to the police?"

She slowly shook her head. "I hadn't gotten around to it." She looked at the door. "Maybe I should now?"

"Too late. Nobody will believe you."

The bell above the door rang, and Steve came in, looked around and came over to our table. His eyes narrowed when he looked at Baz and he slid into the booth beside Jessie. "So what's going on?"

"How'd you find us? You were going to wait at the office."

"You took too long to get back. I returned to the Pelican, and Gerry told me you were here." He nudged Jess. "You okay?"

Jess looked at him, then over the table at me. She sniffed and gave Steve a nudge. "I've got to get out."

Steve acquiesced and watched Jessie leave. He slid back into the booth, looked at Baz, then at me. "Serious. What's happening?"

"Enough circumstantial evidence to sink her and not a single thing she can come up with in her favour." I tapped the table. "Steve-o, you want to be a PI? Come with."

"Where to?"

"Back to where they found Jackson. See what we can see."

Chapter Eleven

Did I mention it was hot? Watching Steve suffer made it almost bearable. He pulled into the parking lot, parked under a tree that would provide shade, until it ignited, got out of the expensive German air conditioning and stepped into hell.

"Where are we going?" Steve flipped the collar of his polo shirt to protect his neck and walked toward the sand.

I rolled up my sleeves and followed. "Top of the wooden steps and left about ten meters."

A gaggle of kids ran up the steps, splitting around us, laughing and hot-stepping over the blistering sand. There was no hope that there would be any evidence left untouched.

The location was pretty easy to see. Crime scene tape fluttered in the light breeze. There was a slight depression in the sand where Jackson had sprawled facedown. Blurry footprints around the depression marked off where the cops and coroner worked. Fuck all else.

"What are we supposed to be looking for?"

I pointed to five metres beyond where we stood. "That's where Jimmy's body was found. Beat to death by two surfer dudes in Jackson's employ." I turned and looked behind us. I pointed at a rock shelf thirty meters away. "And that's where Jackson killed the two surfer dudes. Bang, bang. One each in the back of the head. Too much coincidence here for my liking."

"Jimmy?"

I shook my head and walked to where Jimmy was found. "You wouldn't know him. Young kid worked security at the bank. Long story. Not interested in sharing it." I smiled. "Nice kid, though. Jessie had the hots for him and she fucking near killed me when she found out that Jackson was released from jail."

I turned and looked back. Jimmy died where I stood, Jackson just beyond and the surfers a bit farther.

"You know, if it was just Jimmy and Jackson here, I might actually think Jess had something to do with it. She's very fit and was extremely angry. But in the same place as he shot the other two?" I shook my head. Someone was sending a message.

"So it's like someone is giving the larger criminal community a message, right? Don't mess with whatever family the surfer dudes were part of?"

"Probably." I might have to reconsider the intelligence of this actor guy. "Worth looking into."

We walked back to the parking lot and skirted the table where Jackson attacked me. The shack selling hot food on a hotter day was doing a booming trade in frozen stuff. I doubt they even had the grill on. I leaned on the counter and winked at the middle-aged lady manning the register. "Carol, a couple of those frozen flavoured water things. Too fucking hot out." I looked at Steve. "What colour?"

He patted his flat stomach. "Too much crap in that for me. Can I get a bottle of cold water, Carol?"

She blushed to the roots of her hair. A fan, I

guess. "On the house, Mr Ryan. I loved you in—"

He held up his hand and stopped her, digging a money clip out of his pocket with the other hand. "I couldn't take it for free." He handed over a bill and told her to keep the change.

We sat at the table where I saw Jackson for the last time. "I was thinking the same thing, you know. Someone was pissed off that Jackson killed Baldy and Shaggy."

"The surfers?"

"Yeah. Shaved to a cue ball shine, and the other was a typical long-haired surfer. They tuned me up when I got too close to Jackson during the bank robbery investigation." I rubbed the ribs on my right side. "I didn't realise I was getting too close, but he must have felt I was and sent the monkeys around to warn me off."

"That never works."

"Right." I took too large a bite of the frozen treat and immediately regretted it. I drove my thumb and finger into my eyes. "Son of a bitch. Brain freeze."

Steve laughed. "So if Jackson ran these two 'monkeys', as you call them, why'd he off them?"

"Off them? What is this, the Sopranos? He killed them because they fucked up and drew too much attention to themselves. And too much attention to themselves would lead to too much attention to him. He was afraid. An expedient solution to an annoying problem." I opened my eyes and took a much smaller piece. "That's my assumption, anyway."

"Yeah, well," He took a swig of water, "it caught up with him."

I nodded. "Not a Jessie thing. Problem is, who?"

"It's a small town, Mac. You could probably go through them one at a time and be finished by the weekend."

"If only it were that easy."

"Why couldn't it be?"

I didn't have to answer that. My phone rang. Lily King, calling me. "Mac here. What's up, King?"

"Are you free?" I could hear seagulls and surf in the background. I looked around, expecting to see her.

"Sure. Why not? Where are you?"

"You know the nudie beach?"

"Birdie? Yeah." I looked at Steve. "So, Lily, you getting some sun?"

"My arse. There's a floater up here. Thought you and your ride-along might be interested." There was a brief pause. "It's been in the water a long time. Might be interesting, if you know what I mean."

I chuckled. "You're an evil person, ma'am. We'll be there in ten."

Steve was standing before I hung up the call. "What?"

"A development at Birdie Beach."

"I haven't been there since I was seventeen. Fantastic place."

"You'll be keeping your clothes on this time, bud. King is at the scene of a major development." A body in the water for a long time is a horrible thing to see. Perfect to get shiny boy off his game. I was a little surprised that King wanted to set him up for this, but cops are pretty macabre folks.

There were no trees to park under at the Birdie parking lot; it would be a hot car ride home. We walked down to the beach and took in the sights. There were going to be some bad sunburned butts tonight.

No sight of King, though. I phoned her back and stood at the waterline, trying not to be obvious with my looking.

"Mac? What's taking you so long? We're going to have to pack it up here."

"I'm where you said you were. At Birdie."

"We're at the northern tip of the beach. Hike up here."

I took off my shoes and socks and rolled up my pants. Steve followed suit, and we walked north through the light surf for a few minutes until we saw King and a uniform standing over a seaweed-covered clump of something.

"King. What you got?"

She stood to one side, and I took my first look at the body. It wasn't as bad as I hoped. "Not that long by the look of it."

The body was barely a body. One leg was missing completely, and the other was missing from the knee down. A tattered singlet partially covered the torso, but the ravaged body was still mostly visible. It's not decomposition that gets you when you're in the water; it's the fact that you're a buffet for every creature in the ocean. I cocked my head and looked closer at where the face used to be. Most teeth were missing, but it was impossible to say if that was peri or ante-mortem. The skin was missing in large patches, as was the flesh, exposing large sections of skull.

But there was still some hair. Blond dreads. Familiar looking blond dreads.

"You have a cause of death?"

"Forensic team hasn't touched him yet."

"Bullet to the back of the head, I'd guess. About four months ago. Surprised he looks as good as he does."

King waved a forensic bloke over and squatted by the body's head. "Flip it over. Let me look at the back." She moved out of the way a half step and watched the delicate operation.

I looked over at Steve. His tanned face had faded to a pale, greenish hue, but he hadn't backed up. His sunglasses were off, and he was watching intently as the forensic tech slowly rolled the corpse over onto a rubber sheet.

There *was* a hole in the back of the skull. The

tech moved a few of the dreadlocks to one side and shifted a bit to the left as King squatted beside him.

She looked up at me. "How did you know?"

"The hair. You recognise him?"

She stood and frowned, pulling at an earlobe. "Edge of my memory. You clearly *do* know him."

"Wazza. Warren Montgomery. One of the two fucks that beat the shit out of Jimmy, the bank guard. And one of the two fucks that Jackson shot back where we just were. I would have thought four months in the sea would have done more damage than this."

King scribbled some notes on a pad. "I'm going to have to confirm the identity."

"How? He's got no teeth, fingerprints don't exist when he has no hands, and it's not like he's got a wallet on him."

She squatted and used a pen to move some seaweed out of the way of the upper torso. "DNA from what's left of him, and this octopus tattoo might be enough." She stood. "You say you saw him get shot?"

"Him and his bald buddy." I snapped my fingers. "Jones. Davis Jones. Both of them were shot by Jackson. I testified at Jackson's trial, but there was no concrete evidence other than my word, and every fucking body knows I hated the prick. Thought it was just me being vindictive, I guess."

I think Steve saw enough. He backed off a few steps and turned to face the slight breeze coming in off the ocean. He did better than a lot of rookies I knew.

King tapped her pencil on the notepad. "He was shot back at Budgie?"

I nodded. "And pushed off the rock shelf at the south end of the beach."

"He hasn't travelled far in the past four months. I expect the body was caught under a ledge, away from a lot of the predators. Recent high tide probably jarred him free." She paused and watched the body lifted into a coroner's wagon. "You guys want to come to the morgue with us? We'll find out more there."

"Wouldn't miss it for the world. I'm sure Steve can't wait."

Chapter Twelve

Steve walked back from the surf and slid his sunglasses back on, looking like the cool actor type once again. "Steve can't wait for what?"

"You better? Your colour's coming back."

He smiled wryly. "That was a bit confronting. The last and only dead body I've seen was the open casket at my grandfather's funeral. He looked a little better than that." He looked at the police cars leaving. "You come across that kind of thing very often?"

I could lie. But I didn't. "Not that often. But often enough that you start to develop a callus on whatever part of a man turns him green." I smiled at him. "Pretty ugly, wasn't he?"

"You knew him, I take it."

"Yeah, and he wasn't much better looking when he was alive." I hopped across the hot sand back to the lazy surf. I stood there facing New Zealand. A couple of container ships sat right on the horizon's edge, heading north to somewhere. Steve stood beside me and took a deep breath in through his nose.

"Love that smell."

"If the wind was stronger, that smell would be New Zealand, sheep and cheap wine."

Steve took another deep breath, held it, and then let it out slowly. "I miss this. Peaceful, no annoying fans harassing me, no assistant director yelling at me to get out of the trailer and onto the set."

"And no big bucks. Seriously, mate. I did some checking. You've pulled in some pretty big paycheques your last few jobs." I shrugged. "Not that I've seen anything you do, but, damn. You're worth a pretty sizeable chunk of cash. You can't miss that."

"It comes at a price. It's gotten so that I don't feel like I'm stretching myself anymore. That's the reason I'm following you around, seeing stuff like that body. The next role will take me to new depths, or heights, and I hope the experience here will help." He stole a glance at me. "And instead of parroting someone else's lines, the next one after this one I'm writing. Kind of like Central Coast Underbelly. This is research for that, too." He turned and faced me. "More research for the writing than the upcoming, role, if I'm honest."

"Are you, often?"

"Am I what?"

"Honest."

"Most times."

"Unless you're in front of a camera."

"Most honest then, actually. You have to be true to the part you're playing." He started walking south through the surf. "You've got to tell me what all this is about."

"What, that? The bad guy gets killed, the body eventually washed ashore."

He waved his hand in the air encompassing a larger thing. "Him, Jackson, what happened to this kid named Jimmy you keep talking about? Things are intertwined somehow, Mac. Too many connections."

"It's a small town." It *was* a small town, but I

had been thinking the same thing. Too many connections between these cases that I was starting to wonder about.

"Not that small."

I nodded. "So, from the top?"

"From the top. Research."

"Four months ago, I was asked to cover for the bank guard while the bank prepared for a four-million-dollar money transfer. Physical transfer of physical money. One of those bank transfers with big bags of cash in the back of an armoured truck. Jimmy was supposed to be the guard at the bank, but according to the bank manager on the day, he'd called in sick, and I was hired to sit in for him.

"Then the four million disappeared from the armoured truck, and Jimmy was found pulverised where I showed you. Back near where Jackson was killed."

"Was the money ever recovered?"

"I'll get to that. Jackson was investigating the robbery. I was minding my own business until a quarter million of those four appeared in my account. Then I was in it up to my ass."

"That's a healthy hunk of change."

"I didn't get to keep it if that's what you mean." I stepped around the tendrils of a blue bottle.

"I hired myself to look into the armoured car heist. Sophie worked inside the bank then and helped me out a fair bit. We were getting close to something when Shaggy and his friend Baldy came to call on me and beat the crap out of me as an inducement to stop poking my nose in where they didn't want it."

"Shaggy?"

I hiked my thumb over my shoulder. "That guy. Warren. Did a couple of my ribs."

"You said Jackson ended up shooting him?"

I laughed. "Yeah. Shaggy and his bald buddy were really pissing me off. I saw them in a burger place, annoying a server, and called in a tip, saying they were armed. They got taken in and charged with something or other, but it was enough to tip Jackson over the edge."

"Jackson was always over the edge."

"No argument there. I followed them and Jackson out to Budgie the night they were picked up and watched him shoot them. Blam-blam in the back of their heads."

"I'd heard about the bank robbery. That made the news. I only read the headline, though. Didn't hear about the shootings."

"It was buried pretty deep in the articles about the trial. Jackson's trial," I clarified. "Like I said, I testified to what I saw him doing, but apparently neither the judge nor the jury cared much about what I said I saw. On a dark, moonless night."

Steve laughed. "Surprised you're not a suspect for Jackson's death."

"Oh, King's looking at me pretty hard, and I don't have a good alibi."

"Nobody to vouch for you?"

"Sophie had already left for Newcastle."

"Ex-wife?"

"Jane? Yeah, right. There's no way she'd lie for me, and everybody knows it."

"Small town."

I nodded. "That it is."

"So Jackson was behind the bank robbery? I didn't think he was that smart."

"He wasn't. Harris, the bank manager, had this

hare-brained scheme to set up accounts and transfer money to them, then clean the accounts out later. Then the head office announced a surprise internal audit, and he panicked. Set up a fake transfer, swapped full money bags with stuffed ones and thought he got away with it."

"And you busted it wide open?"

"That I did, sonny." I rubbed my side.

"The bank manager walked?"

I shook my head. "He's still in the slammer. Will be for another decade, I think."

Steve walked with his shoes in one hand and his other hand in his pocket. He looked over at me. "I'm not being obtuse, am I? These killings are all connected."

"In that Jackson killed the guys who killed Jimmy, yeah."

"And whoever killed Jackson didn't place him there by accident. That was intentional. Hell, if I was going to kill someone around here, there are tons of places I could dump the body, and it wouldn't be found for years. The swamp off Ruttlys Road. Or in the bush, fifty metres off the M1. Fucking *nobody* heads in there.

A dead body wouldn't be found for decades. No, Jackson was either killed there or killed somewhere else and moved there for a reason. A message to not fuck with whoever ran Shaggy and Baldy."

I smiled. "You're not too bad at this. You ever get tired of the bags of money and sea of adoring teen-aged female fans, join me. I could use a partner."

"Oh, fuck no. I like the money."

Chapter Thirteen

We walked off the beach to the parking lot. "Ready for the morgue? You're not going to like this." I leaned against his car while he dug out his keys. "The work on the slab gets pretty messy."

"Worse than what we just saw? Perfect. Some reality would do me good. Lead the way."

I shook my head. "The beach was nothing."

"How bad can it be?"

Indeed.

The smell rarely varied: the stench of death with a hint of strong disinfectant. At least that was what it smelled like to my nose, and by the look on Steve's face, even more so for him.

Now, I don't mean it smelled like rotting meat, like a whale carcass on a hot summer beach. But you can tell that there's a dead body on the slab. Bob stood over it, a cup of coffee in his hand, waiting for us to walk over and share the moment with him.

Cleaned up, Shaggy didn't look much better. The left leg was missing in its entirety, separated at the hip bone, and the right was missing from the knee down. The kneecap hung loosely below the femur, a thin piece of skin keeping it attached. Crabs, fish and other sea-based critters had chewed extensively at the flesh. Gender couldn't be determined by sight alone. But I knew who it was. The head was little more than skull, most of the teeth missing and much of the flesh missing from the face. The hair, though, was still there.

I nodded at Bob. "Where's King?"

"She had paperwork to do, I guess. She tells me you know the stiff?"

"One of the Montgomery boys. Warren. Hung with the Davis thug." I pointed at the macabre skull. "I watched the bullet go in. Four months ago. Told all this to King."

"And she told it all to me." Bob finished his coffee and looked for a ledge to place his cup. "It's remarkable how good the shape of this guy is."

Steve stifled a gag. "Good? Looks like something from The Walking Dead."

Bob laughed, pulled on a pair of latex gloves and tossed a pair at me. "Help me out."

I handed the gloves to Steve and he vigorously shook his head, one hand over his mouth and nose, and returned them. "No."

I laughed and pulled on the gloves. 'What are we doing?"

"I have only performed a very preliminary examination. And the body is in such poor shape I need help turning him over." He pointed at the left shoulder. "You lift there, and I'll get him a little lower on the torso."

I will never get used to this. The body was a lot lighter than I expected it to be. Probably because it was missing the legs. And most of the internal organs. The skin that was left slid loosely over the frame and felt like it was going to slough right off. I heard Steve gag. Entertainment wherever I could get it.

Warren's skin was in rough shape. Not enough sunscreen, I guess. And ocean for four months. But it looked like he'd found a sure-fire tattoo removal method. Most of the ink was faded beyond recognition. The skull with a black rose in its teeth was barely there. Not much more than the rose. And a just above it was a constellation of blue dots and the faint outline of an octopus.

I slowly rolled him to his front, and when we were about three-quarters of the way around, his head removed itself from its neck and fell onto the floor.

Steve bolted out the back, retching.

"Oops, my bad, Bob. Should have kept a hold of the noggin." I picked it off the floor and showed him the hole in the back of the skull. "Absolutely positive identification."

Bob sighed and took Warren's head off of my hands. "Warren Montgomery, you say." He placed the head on the slab and pointed at me. "I think you're right. But I'm one hundred per cent not positive. I'll let you know when I am."

I stripped the gloves off. "I'm positive. Confirm it if you want, but there are enough points of identification on this bum for me." I wrinkled my nose. "Smells the same, too."

I stepped outside and unlocked my phone. I hadn't heard from Sophie in a while, unlike her. I dialled the number; there was a brief pause while all of the phone company's electronics sorted things out, and then I was dumped directly into her voicemail. I hung up. I don't listen to other people's messages, so I don't expect people to listen to mine. I thumbed her a quick text message: *"Call me when you can. Hugs to Gwen."*

Steve looked up at me from the step. "Everything okay?"

"I should be asking you that." I slid the phone in my pocket. "You look like shit."

Steve was sitting on the back step, elbows on his knees and head cupped in his hands. The green pallor had returned. I slapped him on the back and sat beside him. "Gritty enough for you? You said you wanted experience. It wasn't that much worse than the beach."

"Fuck, man. That was intense." He took a deep breath. "You have to do that often?"

"Oh, hell no. I hate it. But your reaction was too good." I chuckled as he dry-scrubbed his face. "You'll be able to use it, though, right? That memory will haunt you for a very long time."

"His head bounced."

"Not really. It was more of a thud. And he isn't using it anymore. He wasn't using it much when he was conscious."

"Yeah, that's not going to help the dreams any." He took a deep breath in through his nose and exhaled slowly. "How do you do it?"

"How do I do what?"

He looked over his shoulder at the door, then back to me. "That. And at the beach. Death. A person who is alive one day and a pile of meat the next." He frowned. "Someone you know who's died a violent death like that. How doesn't it affect you?"

"It does. But less and less each time. It's part of the job. Humans are, by and large, dicks. What we're capable of doing to each other doesn't surprise me much anymore." I moved my hand around my torso. "Tons of callouses. All over. Thank god you're an actor. You can fake it. Don't have to actually live it."

"What the fuck was that in there? I've lived it, man."

I laughed. That was rich. "You've experienced a little bit of it. A teeny, tiny little bit of it. Savour it and draw on it when you're on stage." I stood. "You probably couldn't handle much more anyway."

He pushed himself to his feet. "So what now? What are the next steps?"

Always with the hard questions. "This thing was a momentary diversion. Shaggy washing up on shore is a legacy of something four months ago. *He* certainly didn't kill Jackson. So we go back to our job. Shoe leather and working the details. Let's see if King can tell us anything new."

Chapter Fourteen

Steve wiped his face and stood. "Okay." He scratched his jaw. "That was a new experience, Mac. I don't think I'll ever get used to it."

I had a hard time keeping my breakfast down, but he didn't need to know that. I shrugged. "You're lucky." I slapped him on the shoulder. "Can't wait to introduce you to Grange. Looks like he should be breaking bread with Tony Soprano."

I slowed my walk. A couple of familiar and not-that-friendly faces were walking toward us. A couple of Sal's boys. Dick and his ugly friend, Harry. She usually didn't let them off the leash during the day. Steve was a couple of steps ahead of me, oblivious to what he was walking into. Shit. "Steve. Hold up."

He turned back to see what I was talking about just as Dick and Harry reached us. Harry looked like he was carved from granite and had the personality to match. I'd been hit by him in the past. It wasn't pleasant.

Steve found that out when Harry drove a fist into his kidney region. "'Hello, Mac. Who's the pretty? You switch teams?'"

Steve writhed on the ground between us. It looked painful. But to bend down and help was to invite an attack of my own. Mom didn't raise no dummy. "What the fuck, Harry? He's a guest. You didn't have to do that."

"He looked at me funny."

"His back was to you."

Dick stepped over Steve's body and jabbed a finger in my chest. Too easy. He opened his mouth to spout off at me and I grabbed the finger and twisted.

Dick looked like a jacked jockey. Short, but not wiry, with walnuts under his skin. Twisting his finger didn't have the desired effect. He looked at my hand, then up at me, and laughed. And punched me with his weak hand, connecting with that bundle of nerves in the solar plexus that forces your diaphragm to have a seizure.

I grabbed at him as I went down, catching the neck of his filthy T-shirt and tearing the front open. I struggled to get air into my lungs. I tried relaxing. It was the only thing that worked. That and time, and it didn't look like I would get much time.

Harry skipped over and raised a foot to stomp on me. Aiming for the body, so the intent wasn't to kill me. Yet.

I waited for the downswing and rolled away, grabbing his leg. Fuck, I'm stupid. Like granite.

His heel came down on my ribs, a glancing blow, to be sure, along the front, and I'm lucky that's all it did. As I rolled away, he planted that foot and the other followed through with a kick that landed steel-toe first on my shoulder blade.

The pain was enormous. I curled into a ball, fighting nausea and the urge to cry. Pain radiated down the entire left side of my body. And I was lying on my left side.

I heard them laughing about something. Steve was probably getting as much as I was, maybe more. He was a bit of a twat, but he didn't deserve this. I rolled onto my front and tried pushing myself up. I had no strength in my left arm. A small, claustrophobic world swam in front of me. I steadied myself, took a deep breath through my nose and stood. I turned to where Steve had fallen.

He was gone.

Harry and Dick were watching him run away, their backs to me, the shorter Dick on the left and Harry on the right. And I had one of those choices that I always seem to fuck up: I could turn and run the other way, a fairly good chance of getting clear of them for now. An opportunity to regroup, maybe have somebody look at what felt like a broken scapula.

Or I could make the bad decision. Like usually.

I walked toward them as they watched Steve run away. I'm not proud. When attacked by forces stronger in muscle and numbers, sucker punches are absolutely legal.

I sped up, my left arm tucked up against my body to cushion the movement, and let out a yell just as I reached them.

Dick was faster, turning into my fist to his face that stung my hand. Harry reacted the way granite usually reacts, not registering much until Dick stumbled back with his hands on his face.

He should have gone to the ground. I hit him hard enough.

Since I had followed through with the punch, fully committing myself, the logical thing at the time was to pull my arm back and elbow Harry in the side of the head.

It barely rocked him. I was well and truly fucked.

Much of what happened next is a blur of pain. I was out-muscled by sociopaths who were, I'm pretty sure, fully aroused by the time they were finished.

And yet, I was still alive. I looked up at them through swollen eyelids. "Hey, guys, tell Sal that all she had to do was ask for more money for the car. I would have paid it. This wasn't necessary." I rolled to one side and spat with very little force. Bloody spittle dribbled down the side of my face. "But seriously, what was supposed to be the message with this? You'll be wasting a good beating if you forget to give me the message."

Dick's brow furrowed. "Who says there's gotta be a message?"

I tried sitting up—bad idea. "We're all older than 12. You don't fight for fun. If you weren't supposed to give me a message, you'd have just killed me." I took a shuddering breath. "So spit it out. What's the message?"

Harry tapped me on the side of the head with his boot. "Ya gotta stop."

I pushed myself back. "No shit. You don't usually beat the tripe out of someone to make sure they keep doing something. Stop what?"

Dick spat, a wad of phlegm large enough to be self-aware, just missing my head. "Stop helping that bitch what the police say killed Jackson."

They looked at each other, nodded and walked away.

Message delivered.

Chapter Fifteen

I stayed on the ground. Spent a few minutes there, trying to steady my breathing. No point getting up if they were going to come back anytime soon. I was flat on my back, eyes closed, hot as fuck sun burning my face.

I heard footsteps crunching over gravel and opened an eye. I gingerly turned my head and looked in the direction of the noise. If the two arseholes were coming back, I wasn't going to live out the day. I didn't feel like running, but if I had to, I'd find the reserves somewhere.

Fucking white-toothed, blond-tipped Steve swam into view. The arsehole. He saw me and slightly increased his pace.

"Mac? You okay?"

I rolled to my side and got onto my hands and knees. "Where in the hell did you fuck off to?"

"You all right?"

I looked up at him. My left eye was swollen and almost completely shut, and my right was puffed up like Scarlett Johansson's lips. It hurt when I tried a deep breath and I couldn't do anything useful with my left arm. "I'm just fucking awesome. Why'd you piss off? You're in a hell of a lot better shape than I am. I could have used the help. Jesus." I put my hands on my hips and leaned back as far as I could, trying to loosen the tightening muscles. Pain rippled through my body, involuntary spasms jerking me around like a cheap marionette. It's impossible to process thoughts when your brain is focused on all the damaged parts of your body.

Steve looked at his hands, then used one of those manicured paws to scratch at his perfect jawline. "Can't, man. I've got contracts I have to honour. I get my face mashed up, and my career is over. And my hands." He shook his head. "No. Can't get into any fights. Sorry, Mac." He cocked his head and looked at my face. "We should get you to a hospital."

I shrugged and winced. "Not necessary. Drive me back to my place, okay? I've got some pain medication. And some ice." I fished my phone out of my pocket. The screen was cracked. Those fuckers would pay. I scrolled through the recent contacts and found Alfie's number.

"What's up, Mac?"

"A couple of Sal's boys just tuned me up. A warning to stay away from and I quote, 'that bitch what killed Jackson.' Let Jess's parents know. But don't tell Jess whatever you do."

"You know who they were? I'll call the cops for you."

Oh, fuck no. "Don't. Not yet. It'll exacerbate the situation and I don't need any exacerbating going on right now. Just give Gerry a heads up, okay?"

"Are you okay?"

"I'll live. Which in and of itself is a bit of a surprise, don't you think? They left me alive and able to identify them. They aren't worried about any comeback."

"Bullshit. You know who they are, you tell me and I'll arrange for them to get picked up."

"No exacerbating, mate. Leave it be for now." I hung up and put the phone in my pocket. Steve-o, where are you parked again?"

Young Cameron didn't look up from the screen when I walked in, but Lincoln wagged his arse end like he hadn't seen me in months. I gave him a pat on the head and got right up close to Cameron before I talked. "Hey, kid. You find Betty yet?"

"Whazzat?" He poked a couple of more keys, then looked up at me. "Jesus." He pushed his chair back, away from me and into the wall. "What the fuck happened to you?" He looked past me like my assailants were coming through the door behind me. "You look like hell."

"So, no Betty?"

He stared at me for a second, then eased back to the computer. "I've hacked every loyalty card database I can think of. There's been no activity from her on any of them for a couple of weeks. The ones she has, that is. She doesn't have many."

"She's rich. She doesn't need loyalty cards. Maybe that's not the best use of your time." I scribbled a number on a piece of paper. "This is Sophie Patterson's mobile number. I haven't heard from her in a couple of days, which is not normal for her. I'm starting to get concerned. It's going straight to voicemail. Can you do something with the phone company or something to track down her latest location?"

Cameron looked at the number. "It wouldn't happen to be an Apple product, would it?"

"That helps?"

"It would. Might." He handed the paper back to me. "Could you write down any email addresses she might have?"

"That would help, too?" I wrote down the only one I knew.

"Can't hurt." Cameron took the paper back from me. "I'll see what I can do."

"Text me if you find out anything."

I went into the loo, dropped a couple of those serious painkillers and washed it down with water. I looked at myself in the mirror and took a step back. I looked like hell. No wonder the kid jumped. I smiled, and that made it worse.

I moved my left arm away from my body and a sharp pain took my breath away. Shit.

I pointed at Steve as I left the bathroom. "You're right. Take me to the hospital. Something doesn't feel right."

"Something doesn't look right, either. Your face looks like an untalented kid formed it out of clay."

I stifled a laugh. "Thanks, pretty boy. You know where the hospital is?"

"I've been there."

Cameron held up his hand. "Um, Mac, what about Betty?"

It was getting too hard juggling all the stories and I needed someone to look at my fucking back. Jesus. "You're not going to find her with loyalty cards or library cards. Take a step back and think outside the box." I offered a wan smile. "Try thinking like a rich woman in her fifties. What would you do in her shoes if you wanted to hide?"

"Why'd she want to hide?"

I pointed at him smiled. "Exactly. Do some

asking around and see what you can find out. Tell anyone who asks you're working on my behalf." I pointed at my face. "I've got to see a guy about this, or it'll stay this way."

Steve held the door for me and closed it behind us. "Where's Betty?"

"Don't worry about her. Her husband hired me to find her." I smiled. "And she's paying me to stay hidden. For a little while, anyway."

He chuckled. "Cameron doesn't know, though, right?"

"Nah. But I'm paying him well. He won't find her, though."

"And Sophie Patterson?"

"Different story. She left to visit her sister in Newcastle a couple of days ago, and I haven't heard from her since. Very unlike her." I walked down the stairs on the outside of my building, holding on to both handrails, walking like my grandfather did when he shat himself.

"Two days isn't that long."

"It is for her." I eased myself into Steve's car. "Two or three calls a day, usually."

"Probably forgot to take her phone charger with her, and it's dead. Happens to me all the time."

I shrugged and immediately regretted it. "If that's the case, fine. Better safe than sorry." I pointed forward. "To the hospital, James."

Chapter Sixteen

The waiting room was lightly populated, fortunately, because I was in no mood. Steve badgered me about Sophie the entire trip, like it was some high school romance thing.

"Listen, mate, leave it alone, okay?"

He looked at me. "Okay."

"Okay."

A triage nurse came into the waiting area and called my name. "Durridge. Room 1.3, please."

"Take off if you want, Steve. I can get a lift back."

"Oh, hell no. I'm waiting for you. You can't get rid of me that easy." He leaned back in his chair and laced his fingers behind his head. "I'll people watch. It's a thing we actors do. One day, I might have a part where I need to wait."

I sat in room 1.3 and made myself as comfortable as I could. It was: wait to get a room, then wait for the doc to show up once you got the room. And if he didn't show up in ten, I was walking. The arm was feeling better, although that was probably due to the pills I had already taken.

I had just settled in and the door opened. What a pleasant surprise. Beating my expectations. I turned awkwardly in my seat to make some kind of crack and groaned.

"Hi, Mac. What brings you here today? You've pissed someone off, I see."

Jane. My former wife, and now an intern at the hospital. Still looking good, too. She'd cut her hair short, and it suited her. What a royal pain in the arse. "Why you?"

She smiled like she was really enjoying herself. "Chart says you've been on the receiving end of a bit of a beating. No way I'd miss this. Hop up on the table and take your shirt off."

Jane and I had been married for twelve years. Mostly good, I thought, but she didn't. At the tail end of our relationship, she finished a degree she had been working on and got into med school just before the divorce. My monthly support payments funded her lifestyle. Visits like this made me want it to happen all that much faster.

"There'll be no hopping today." I eased my shirt off and started to move onto the table when Jane stopped me and looked at my back.

"That must hurt."

"I hurt all over. Can you be more specific?"

She tapped my left shoulder blade with a gloved finger, and I jumped. "That. A boot?"

"A couple of boots. Is it broken?"

She stood behind me and took my left wrist in her hand and slowly raised my arm out to my side. "Does that hurt?"

"Like a son of a bitch. And you're enjoying it."

"Be nice, Mac." She poked my shoulder blade. "This isn't broken—bad bruise. You look like you were used as a piñata. What is it this time?"

I pulled my shirt back on. "Nothing you need

to concern yourself with. Thanks for the visit. It was swell."

She put her hand on the middle of my chest. "Hang on, cowboy. Sit up there and let me look at your face."

"You hitting on me?"

"You wish."

I eased onto the padded table, and she slid in between my legs to get a closer look. She reached behind me, pulled a couple of latex gloves from a box and snapped them on. In the process of getting the gloves, she pressed herself tight into my crotch, and my crotch had a long memory.

I gently took her hips, paused for a second, and pushed her a few centimetres away. "Don't fuck with my head, Jane. It's not nice."

The grin was evil. There was a day, many days, in the past when that grin was a precursor to light wrestling, rolling around in cooperative play and, depending on the day, either rapid or slow, languorous, sexy time. But those days were well behind us.

She broke open a sterile pack and poured some distilled water on it. "This might sting." She dabbed at a cut on my cheekbone. She was right. It did sting. A lot. "This is going to need to be closed up."

"No stitches, please."

"It's not the dark ages. And it's not that deep. You look like you've been on the losing end of a cage fight."

"Yeah, you should see the other guys."

"More than one?"

"Not your concern, I told you."

She frowned at me and tore open a dressing. "Should I be alerting the police that I have with me what appears to be the victim of a violent crime?"

"You'd be wasting your time." I winced as she stuck a plaster of some sort on my cheek.

"Stop moving."

"Stop acting like you enjoy giving out pain."

She shook her head and took stock of the rest of my face. I couldn't tell what she was looking at. Bruises, I guess. Some places she poked felt spongy and hurt when she touched them. She took another surgical pad, distilled water, and wiped clean more, smaller abrasions on my face. Then, she applied some type of antibacterial cream to the better part of my face.

If my face had a better part.

She was wiping away a last bit of cream and brushed across my right eyebrow and I almost went off the back of the table.

"Son of a bitch, Jane. What the fuck?"

"Potty mouth. I think it's a bit worse than I thought."

"You think?" I gingerly touched the eyebrow. Squishier than I expected it to be, and a slicing spear of pain brought tears to both of my eyes. "Broken?"

"Fracture, I suspect. Not completely broken. Don't touch it again."

"Oh, fucking trust me. I won't. What do you do for it?"

She snapped her gloves off and looked at me like I was a few beers short of a slab. "We're going to put a cast on your face," she said. "What do you think? Nothing. Pain pills, and don't bump it. Give it a month. Don't let anyone punch you in the head for a while."

"It's not like I asked him to. And I'm pretty sure it wasn't a punch. More like a boot."

"Even more so, then." She swept the detritus from her first aid into a medical waste bin and watched me slide off the table. "So, what have you gotten yourself into?"

I opened my mouth to respond when the examination door opened, and the triage nurse poked her head in. "Someone here to see Mac."

"I'm not finished. I think he's got a fractured eye socket. Tell them to wait."

The door was pushed open, and Grange and a uniform walked in.

"Hey, Grange. What's going on?

"Malcolm Durridge, you're going to come downtown and chat with us about some aspects of Jackson's death.

"No can do, man. Doc's still working on me."

Grange looked at my face, winced at what he saw, and said, "You'll live."

I stood in front of him with my wrists together out in front of me. He stared at me for a full minute, squinted, and then shook his head. "Not unless you force me to. You're not under arrest, but we need to talk to you. Now."

I walked through the waiting room with Grange in front and the uniform behind me. I caught

Steve's eye and gave him a short shake of my head. He eased back into his chair and watched me leave, sandwiched between the uniform and Grange.

Grange opened the back door of the marked police car, and the uniform—Warburton by the name on his shirt—pushed my head to one side and bumped my face on the edge of the door opening.

"Fucking hell, mate. Can't you see my face? Fractured eye socket. Jesus." The pain seared and I fought the urge to vomit. "Was that really necessary?"

I eased into the back seat on my own. Warburton was saying something that sounded appropriately apologetic, but I wasn't paying much attention to the words.

Grange just grunted and opened his car door. "Get him to the station, Warburton. Don't fucking kill him on the way."

Chapter Seventeen

I'd been in this particular interrogation room many times, but not on this side of the table.

I was on my own, sitting in a chair on one side and facing two chairs on the other side. Thanks to the bruised scapula and fractured eye socket, there was a dull throb on the entire left hand side of my body. It was not a good day overall.

I'd never taken much notice of the inside of the room before. It was just a secure place to isolate a suspect and question them for as long as it took. The difference between a cop and a perp in an interrogation room is that the cop gets overtime. He'd stay there all day and night if he felt it would advance a case.

Sometimes, when there were bills to pay, he'd sit there even if he knew it *wouldn't* advance a case.

I wasn't a typical perp, though. I knew the game. I was one of the best at playing the game. Grange was dreaming if he thought he'd get anything out of me.

Primarily because there was nothing to get out of me. I didn't kill Jackson. Sure, I've dreamt about it. Fantasised about it. Never acted on it. I'm not an idiot.

I settled myself in the chair. Made myself as comfortable as I could, given the bruises and the cheap furniture. The interrogator's chairs were much more comfortable than the metal one I was sitting in.

Grange had the temperature cranked down as low as the system allowed. Not that I was complaining. It was a nice contrast to the blast furnace outside.

I was settling into the space when the door swung open, and Grange and King walked in. King sat across from me to my left and Grange to my right. Grange took out a digital recorder, placed it on the table in front of us and turned it on. He cleared his throat. Looked over at King and opened a small notebook.

"Malcolm Durridge, do you need us to provide you with an attorney?"

"What in the hell would I need an attorney for? I'm not under arrest. I haven't broken any laws. I certainly didn't kill Jackson. If I had, you'd never find the fat, stinking corpse."

King leaned into the table. "You realise that you are not obliged to say or do anything unless you wish to do so, but whatever you say or do may be used in evidence, right? Do you understand?"

I waved it away. "I spent more years on that side of the table than either one of you have. Almost more than the two of you combined. I know exactly what my rights are. And since I'm not under arrest, you can both go fuck yourselves."

Grange stared at me like I hadn't said a word. "Why did you kill Jackson?"

"I thought you said Jessie killed him?"

"She would have needed help. No way she could do it herself."

"So your argument is to pile on. Well, she didn't do it, and I didn't do it. Either separately or together. Wrong guy, wrong gal."

"Mac, we've confirmed that the cord used to strangle Jackson came from Jessie's leg rope. Her epithelial cells are on the ends of the cord, and his are in the middle, where it was wrapped around his throat. She most likely couldn't have subdued him first, and that's where you come in."

"Oh, that's absolute horseshit. You're piecing together something convenient out of nothing. Of course, her trace would be on the cord. It's her cord. You've got nothing."

"Not nothing, Mac. Plenty. There's ample physical evidence, and if you recall, I was present in the parking lot when she threatened to kill him. And you are still pissed off about him walking after putting him in jail. Not your favourite guy, right? You made some threatening statements yourself after that Jessie girl left the beach. Launched yourself over the picnic table and took a swing at him. Motive, means, opportunity."

"Horseshit." I ignored Grange and looked at King, sitting there, saying nothing and looking concerned. "Do you believe this?"

"I don't want to, Mac. But I'm having a hard time coming up with any other possibilities."

"You're not trying hard enough." I stood and paced the small room. I stopped in front of the table and looked down at them. "This is going to sound really clichéd, but while you're wasting your time with Jessie, and apparently me, the real killer is walking free."

"Sit down, Mac. We haven't finished talking."

I stared at Grange for a minute, then pulled the chair back and sat. Leaned my elbows on the table, rested my head in my hands and looked at him. "So, what other shit do you want to spread?"

"What were you doing the night Jackson was murdered?"

I sat back and dropped my hands on the table. "So am I under arrest?"

"We're just hoping you'll cooperate and avoid that, Mac," said King.

I held out my wrists again. "Arrest me, or I'm leaving."

Grange cleared his throat and slowly stood. "If you insist."

The door to the interview room was flung open, and Steve walked in, in a suit and tie and wearing a pair of ridiculous Clark Kent-y glasses. "Mr Durridge, don't say anything." He turned to Grange. "Unless you plan on arresting my client, we're walking out of here. Now."

Grange was turning shades of red. "Who the fuck do you think you are, Matlock? Of course, he's free to go. He's not under arrest. He was helping us with some questions. Could have left any time he wanted, you fucking wanker."

King had a small smile on her face and an arched eyebrow.

I gave Steve a bit of a shove as we walked toward the door. "How did you get in?"

He laughed. "Security in here is ludicrous. Come on. We're leaving." He hammered on the door and a uniform opened it. Steve held it for me as I walked out.

"Later, Grange. Do some real work. Find out what really happened. Stop wasting your time on a young girl and an ex-cop."

I walked through the door, Steve on my heels. We made good time and exited the station before Grange changed his mind.

"What the fuck was that, Steve?" I laughed and gave him another shove. "A lawyer?"

"I played one a few years ago. Criminal defence attorney." He took off the glasses. "Look, plain glass." He laughed. "Do you think they bought it?"

"Fuck, no." I laughed again. "Definitely not your babysitter. King was having a hard time not laughing. You're fucking insane, you know that?"

He clawed at the tie, removed it and the suit jacket and them it over his shoulder. "How do people wear these all the time? In this heat?" He slapped me on the back and pulled his hand back when I winced. "Shit. Sorry. You okay?"

I eased my left arm around in a small circle. "I'll live."

"Again, sorry. So what do we do next? These guys full-on think you and Jessie did this."

"And you know we didn't?"

He smiled. Gently, this time, he placed his hand on my shoulder. "No way in hell, mate." We walked a few steps. "Seriously, Mac. What do we do next? We've got to do something or you'll end up in the slammer."

Tony McFadden

156

Chapter Eighteen

He was right. I had to head this off before I needed Alf to defend me. "So let's look at the facts. Somebody killed Jackson."

"True."

"And someone did their best to make it look like Jessie did it." I looked around. "Where'd you park? I'm not walking all the way back."

"Around the corner. Do you think whoever did this intentionally targeted Jessie? Or was it just bad luck on her part?"

I shrugged, immediately regretting it. Slow and steady for a little while. "Don't know."

We got into his car, and he pointed it toward The Pelican. He asked, "So, how do you track someone's activity?"

"Normally I talk to the last person I know he was with, but that was Grange, and Grange isn't being very cooperative right now." I tugged at my earlobe. "So second best is we do a walk around town and see what we can find out. See if anybody saw him that afternoon and evening."

"So, like walking door-to-door. In this heat."

I chuckled. "Toughen up, kiddo. It's good for character."

"I've been more characters than you can count."

"Smart-arse."

"Seriously. All ends of the spectrum. And I take it seriously, Mac. Research as much as I can. Played a cop, lawyer - you're welcome - bank robbers, taxi drivers, beach bums, gay porn star, drover. You name it, I've done it."

I looked over at him. "How? You're fucking, what, twenty? How can you have done that much?"

"Thirty. Almost." He shrugged. "And sure,

some of them were bit parts, but I researched them just as much. No point doing a job unless you're doing it right."

"You're exhausting me just listening to you."

"Toughen up, gramps."

"Go fuck yourself."

He laughed. "So where do we start? Where does he normally hang around?"

I thought for a second. Shook my head. "That's not where we're going. Turn around."

"Back to the beach?" He hit a traffic circle and took the fourth exit.

"We'll start there."

We parked in almost the same place Grange had pulled his car on the day Jackson was killed. Steve turned off the ignition, and as soon as the air conditioning stopped, the heat started seeping through the glass. And it was pushing 5:00 p.m.

He jacked the door open. "It's like an easy-bake oven in here. What are you waiting for?"

Late-afternoon and the pavement was still soft from the heat. Steve made a bee-line for the food counter. He was a natural. I arrived just after him and heard him ask, "So, what time did Jackson leave here?"

Maybe not a natural. The lady behind the counter had a look on her face like she wanted to eat Steve. I looked at him. I could see it, I guess. Good looking man. Stood out too much, though.

I knocked on the counter to get her attention. "There was an unmarked police car here two days ago. Grange got out with a fat, greasy bum of a man and sat at that table." I pointed near the car. "They bought some burgers and drinks."

She was nodding. "Yeah. A couple of double cheeseburgers. Both of them got drinks, too."

"Great. Did they leave together?"

She shook her head. "The cop left alone," she said. "I think he got a call on his radio. He left in his car and turned left, like he was heading to Gosford. The fat guy stayed at the table, ate his burger, then finished what was left of Grange's."

Steve leaned in like he was taking her into his confidence. "We're trying to piece together that fat, greasy man's timeline. Do you remember the registration of the vehicle that picked him up?"

She looked confused for a second. "Nobody picked him up. He walked."

"Are you sure?" I asked. "He wasn't in the greatest shape."

"It was busy here, but I wouldn't forget that. I remember thinking he was going to die of heat stroke before he got anywhere."

"Did he go the same way as Grange?"

"No, the other direction. If you're looking for him, he's probably in the hospital, recovering."

"He wasn't so lucky." Steve nodded toward the beach. "He ended up dead up on the sand."

She grabbed the front of her t-shirt. "Oh, my god. That was him?"

I nodded and turned to leave. "It was. Let's go, Steve. Dead end here."

He patted the woman's hand and followed. "Maybe there are traffic cameras on the road. We can see who picked him up."

"This isn't C.S.I. And there isn't enough traffic on the road to warrant a camera. And even if there was, how do you think I'd be able to get my hands on the footage?" I shook my head. "Dead end." I stopped at the car. Steve kept walking to the road.

"Are you even going to look?" he asked. And he continued walking toward the road.

"Fuck." The pavement was hot under my Volleys, and I really didn't feel like a walk. But he had a point. Better to check and confirm than guess. I broke into a slow trot and caught up to him. I was drenched with sweat by the time I got there. Ten steps. Soaked.

I scanned the tops of the light standards in both directions. No cameras, as I expected. I waved my arm expansively from North to South. "See? No cameras."

"Really?" Steve pointed at a white mobile speed camera vehicle sitting on the far side of the road, its camera visible through the back glass window.

"Mate, that's a speed camera. Do you know what the odds are of it grabbing a photo of a speeding car with Jackson just happening to be walking down the road? Extremely slim. A pic that happens to show him getting into someone else car? Even slimmer."

"Worth a check though, right? Who do we talk to?"

"Private contractors ran these trucks. I might know a guy who knows a guy." I tapped him on the shoulder and headed back to his car. "Don't hold your breath, though."

We parked behind the office. "Are we going to walk the businesses and see if we can track his movement?"

I looked at Steve. "You were the one complaining about the heat not even two hours ago. Now you want to go out in the middle of it? We're heading up and getting a bite first. Maybe a drink. Or two."

"Pussy."

I laughed and closed his car door a little harder than I needed to. I walked up the stairs, ignoring whatever it was he was saying. I'd get Cameron to contact the guy who operated the mobile speed cameras and see if he could share with us whatever photos he got the afternoon Jackson was walking on the road, but I didn't hold out much hope.

I opened the door and stepped into my office and the cool air the air-con provided. Cameron was head down and hard at work at something. Betty, I guess. I was going to have to bring that to an end soon. I pushed past the door and saw Sophie, her back to me, looking at a picture on the wall.

"Sophie. I've been trying to reach you. Your phone is busted, I think."

Steve walked in behind me as she turned. It wasn't Sophie. It was Gwen. The same height, up to my chin. She had the same dark hair down to her shoulders. Same dark, permanently tanned skin. From the back, indistinguishable from her older sister. From the front, Gwen wore glasses and had a slightly wider face. Easy to tell. "Shit, Gwen. What are you doing here?"

"Is Sophie here? I need to talk to her."

"No. She left yesterday to visit you."

"I just got here. She didn't arrive."

"Have you heard from her at all?"

Gwen shook her head. "Not today. She called yesterday and said she was on the way, then nothing." She glanced at Steve, ignored him, then back at me. "I'm worried. Can you help me find her?"

Chapter Nineteen

I took out my phone and called Sophie. Again. Same result. The call went directly to voicemail. And I tried again. Same result. Definition of insanity, right?

"Yes. Definitely. You don't even have to ask. Sit. We need to talk. You need to tell me everything you know. Can I get you something to drink?"

Steve pressed down on my shoulder. "I'll get something cold for both of you."

Gwen watched him move into the kitchen. "That's the guy from—"

"Yup. Long story. Go with it." I took a breath. "When did you talk to her last? And where was she?"

She was shaking her head before I finished

talking. "She called me just after she left. Left here, I assume. She told me she was on the way and that we would drink our troubles away. I didn't hear from her after that."

Cameron stood from the desk. "I need to go, man. I need to get my mum at work. You want me back here tomorrow?"

I was going to cut him loose after today, but I had an actual missing persons case now. "Back by 9:00 tomorrow morning, okay?"

"Sure thing, Mac." He slid out the door, letting in a wave of heat as he left.

I waited for the door to close and took drinks from Steve. I took a sip. Non-alcoholic, by the taste. Arsehole actor. "Gwen, you hungry? Let's head across the street and get some food. Steve is buying."

Jessie was working, which was surprising. If I had been charged with murder and out only by good luck and a good lawyer, I'd be holed up in my room, getting permanently soused. She dropped menus on our table, eyes glued to Steve.

"Take your time, Steve. Hi, Mac. Hi, Sophie."

Eyes never left Steve. She turned and walked back to the kitchen before Gwen or I had a chance to correct her.

"She seems a bit star-struck." Gwen had a slight smile on her face. "You normally have this effect on people, Mr Ryan?"

Steve sported a blush. "Most people. Not you, apparently. Not a fan?"

"I was when I was much younger."

"Ouch. I'm going to get some beer, Mac. You two want?"

I nodded and turned my focus to Gwen. "Sophie. She told me she was heading to help you sort out some domestic issues."

"We were going to eat ice cream and drink wine. So, yeah, I guess that's sorting out domestic issues." She sat back in her seat. "But she didn't show."

"Why did you wait for two days to do anything?"

"Thought maybe she changed her mind. But that's not like her."

Steve returned with the schooners of beer, sliding them in front of us. "So, what's up?"

"Just shush, Steve. We're busy." I turned my attention back to Gwen. "She said you guys didn't talk much with your brother."

"Stan? Fuck no. I love him, like the way you always love a sibling, but he is his own worst enemy. He got into trouble a long time ago and stayed there. Wrong crowd, wrong decisions, not a life I'm willing to acknowledge. If he ever sincerely asks for help, I'll help, but it will be with a tonne of conditions."

"More info than I was looking for. Any chance Sophie connected with Stan?"

She shook her head. "Unlikely. Her feelings were stronger than mine. Are stronger than mine. She's okay, right?"

I didn't say anything. I had no idea if she was alright, and I really wanted to know. There hadn't been a single time in the past five months that she'd gone off the grid without letting someone know where she was. I only knew her a small percentage of her life, though, so I didn't know what she was like before we met.

"I'm worried, Mac. She spoke a lot about you. It's not like her to stay out of contact this long. Really not like her."

That answered that. "What's the longest she's been out of touch, as far as you know?"

She shook her head, thinking. "I don't know. If you include Facebook and Instagram posts, never more than a day. Never."

Jessie arrived to take our orders, but we hadn't even looked at the menus yet.

"Not ready yet, Jess."

Steve jumped in. "Bring us a large vegetarian pizza on a gluten-free base, okay? And if you've got dairy free cheese, that would be awesome."

Fucking actors. I waved assent to Jessie and turned back to Gwen. "I'm worried, too. Does she have any other friends in Newcastle that she might have gone to?"

"Not without touching base with me."

I took out my phone. "Have you talked to the police?"

"In Newcastle. To no avail. They talked about her being an adult, free will, no signs of forceful removal from anywhere, just a big pile of bullshit."

I unlocked my phone and scrolled through the

contacts. "I'll give it a shot." I found the name I was looking for and poked the "Call" button.

Grange answered after the second ring. "I'm off duty, Mac. What can I do for you?"

"You're on speaker, Willy. I've got Sophie's sister with me, Gwen."

"Hi, Gwen. What can I do for you guys?"

She leaned into the phone. "My sister went missing two days ago. She was driving from Mac's place here in town to my place in Newcastle and she never made it."

There was quiet on the line. Then, "Have you notified the police in Newcastle?"

"I did. They said they can't do anything. She's an adult and can go where she wants. She doesn't have to tell anyone, but I know she's missing. She's not just off on her own somewhere. She was coming to visit me to commiserate with me about my failed marriage."

"They were correct in what they said. There really is nothing the police can do. If she were twelve, that would be different, but she's an adult. Free to go where she wants. If I were you, I'd check with the Highway Patrol to see if there was an accident on the way. Or check the hospitals between here and there. It's not currently a police matter. Hopefully, she shows up and it won't become a police matter. I'm about to sit down to dinner, so I'm going to let you go. Best of luck with your search."

He hung up.

"What the hell was that?" asked Gwen.

I shrugged. "He's right, unfortunately." I slid the beer closer to her. "Have a sip. We'll find her. I've got an idea." I waved Jessie over. "Jess, when the pizza is ready, make it to go, okay? We've got to head back to the office."

I sat in front of the computer and launched the browser. I headed to the site that let me find my phone if it was lost. I knew Sophie's email. We'd have to guess her password.

I typed in the email address and sat back in the chair. "We need her password. Any ideas?"

"Let me in there." Gwen pushed me to one side and sat at the desk. She rummaged through the dozens of sticky notes, scraps of paper and scribbled-on margins. She looked at each one for a second, then tossed it to one side. The pile grew until she stopped, stuck the piece of paper on the edge of the monitor and typed.

A compass oscillated for a few seconds, then a representation of Sophie's phone appeared on the screen. Gwen clicked on the phone icon, opening a map. Small red text beside the phone icon reported "Old Location" and the date and time about an hour and a half after she had left my place, two days ago.

I leaned close. "Zoom out a bit." Gwen spun the wheel on the mouse and expanded the view. I tapped on the screen. "I know that place. About a block away from the shopping centre in Kotara."

I stuffed a piece of pizza in my mouth, forcing myself to chew and swallow. Beggars can't be choosers. It was horrible, but it was food. "I'm heading up there. See what I can see."

Gwen stood. "I'm going with."

"I'm driving," said Steve.

"And I'm getting some takeaway that doesn't taste like cardboard."

I put the rest of the pizza in Lincoln's dish. "Don't hate me, dog."

Chapter Twenty

Steve hopped into his car and Gwen and I stood next to it.

"What?"

I looked at the one remaining seat, then at Gwen. "So which of us stays?"

"Damn." He hopped back out. "What are you driving, Gwen?"

Gwen drove. I sat in the front passenger seat, and Steve sprawled across the back seat. The drive in her Toyota rental was uneventful. The sun was down, and the temperature was getting back below pizza oven levels. Traffic was light. We travelled in silence for a bit. I watched Gwen drive. She had the same fine muscles in her arms as Sophie, slight twitches as she controlled the wheel up the Pacific Highway. We were cruising along nice and quiet. I could almost catch a wink or two.

Then Steve spoke from the back. "Is Kotara near where you live, Gwen?"

"Not really. I suppose if traffic was bad on the Inner City Bypass, you could duck through Kotara to get to where I lived, but it would have added time to the trip overall."

"So no real reason for her to go there?"

I turned around in my seat. "You're a detective now? She just said that it would be a way to go if traffic was bad on the main drag."

He put up his hands in surrender. "Fine, fine. I'll leave it to you. You're the pro."

Didn't make me feel any better. I was winging it.

Forty minutes into the drive and the blue flashing dot on my phone was within a block of where Sophie's phone last updated. "Slow down, Gwen. We're close."

Steve stirred. He yawned and leaned forward,

looking over the seatback at my phone. "Here's as good a place as any, right?"

I nodded. "Pull over anywhere, Gwen." There were fast food joints, pizza places, a couple of service stations and a 24-hour convenience store, all within walking distance. "Steve, I'm going to send you a picture of Sophie."

I selected a good headshot and sent it to him. Gwen parked at the curb by an intersection, and we got out of her car. She gave both of us her phone number, and she logged Steve's.

"Okay, meet back here," I said. "Check every open place. See if they saw Sophie on Monday and if they have any information about her. And keep an eye out for her car, just in case. It's a two-year-old red Honda Civic."

"What's the registration?" asked Steve.

"No idea. Sorry." I pointed west. "I'll head this way. Call me if you discover anything."

We all bumped fists. It was a spontaneous thing that made me feel weirdly uncomfortable, but the other two took it very seriously, like we were embarking on a quest. Which I guess we were.

I stopped at a service station and showed the clerk the picture on my phone. The tag on his shirt said his name was Ahmad.

"Did you see this woman on Monday, Ahmad? She was wearing a light blue sundress with pale yellow flowers on it."

Ahmad shook his head. "No luck, mate. I wasn't working on Monday. Monday and Tuesday off. I work the weekend. Rajiv was working Monday." He pointed at the picture on my phone. "And he's got a great memory for good-looking ladies. He'll be in after midnight if you want to talk to him."

I looked at my watch. Five hours. "Maybe I'll drop by." I looked at the cameras in the ceiling. "Would you—"

"No joy there. I don't have access to the video. It goes back to a central monitoring place, they say, but I don't believe them. They probably don't even work." He shrugged. "Sorry. If I see her, I'll tell her you're looking for her." He picked up a pen. "What's your name?"

"Don't worry about it. I'll stop by later."

It was going to be a long night.

I had just as much luck at a franchise burger place, a franchise chicken place, an indie pizza place and a bowling alley. Nobody knew nothin'. But I got myself a slice of pizza that more than made up for the crap Steve fed me.

It took me almost two hours to travel three blocks, talking to every open joint. A few thought they may have seen her walking. One guy at a TAB betting office thought he saw her getting into a Volkswagen Microbus.

I had resigned myself to a wasted night when I walked around the corner and saw her car. I checked the doors. Unlocked. I slid into the driver's seat and reached across to the glove box. As I went through it, I saw the key ring I had given her on her birthday three months earlier sitting on the console. It was unmistakable. A pair of dolphins attached by a sturdy chain to a ring. It was her car. And a testament to the honest folks of Kotara that it hadn't been stolen in the past three days. I sent text messages to Gwen and Steve: "Meet me back at the car, ASAP."

I pushed the ignition button and the car

started. Lights on, seatbelt fastened and I made it back the three blocks in five minutes. I parked behind Gwen's car and got out, leaning against Sophie's car, waiting for them to walk back.

I wasn't feeling good about this. She never left the keys in the car. She'd never leave the car parked on the side of the road for this long. I checked the body for scrapes or dents. It took a long time to check. Carefully. Nothing appeared to be out of order.

Gwen came around the corner and Steve crossed the street at almost the same time. Gwen noticed the car first.

"Sophie's?"

I nodded and patted the fender. "It was three blocks west of here. The phone dies around here. So something made her get out of her car, leave the keys behind and then head this way. Not long after, her phone is disabled."

Steve had a concerned look on his face. "Shouldn't you have left it for the cops to process? You know, fingerprints and stuff like that."

"Cops aren't treating her as missing." I thought about what to do next. "None of the people I talked to saw her. Like she was invisible. You guys have any luck?"

Gwen shook her head.

"I did, I think," said Steve. "A guy by the name of Bruce saw a woman that looked like her in the back seat of an old Holden early Monday afternoon, but he can't swear to it."

"So nothing," said Gwen.

I found Cameron's phone number in my contacts and called him.

"Mac?"

"Do me a favour, will you? When you get in tomorrow, keep pinging Sophie's number on the phone finding site."

"I don't have the credentials."

I gave him the email address and password and made sure he had it right. "We're going to be staying up here tonight and canvassing the area again in the morning. Let me know as soon as something comes up."

"How do I get into your office?"

"You can do this from home, right? I'll still pay you. You don't need to be at my desk."

"Yeah. Sure." He paused for a second. "What about the Betty thing? Am I still looking for her?"

Shit. I forgot about that. "Leave it with me for now. Just focus on Sophie. Okay?"

The kid agreed and hung up. I looked at Gwen. "I don't want to impose. We can stay in a hotel. Will you join us for breakfast?"

She smiled. "My place isn't big enough to accommodate two adult males if I'm not sharing a bed with them. The hotel sounds good."

Steve cocked an eyebrow, and I elbowed him in the ribs. "You're having dinner with us, though. Do you know any good places around here?"

Chapter Twenty-One

Steve sprung for a couple of huge rooms at a hotel on the Pacific Highway. We checked in, then the three of us headed to the hotel's bar and grill. Gwen got some kind of healthy salad thing, Steve ordered a fish dish and I ordered a steak. Beer for me, sparkling water for his highness and white wine for Gwen.

Drinks came first, and we started spit-balling about the whereabouts of Gwen's sister and my live-in partner.

"Was she upset about something before she left?" asked Gwen.

"About your situation. She was down on men as a species. And she was very eager to visit you, commiserate, eat ice cream and drink wine."

"She seemed pretty upbeat when she called me on Monday."

"Remarkable. She was ready to bite my head off when she left. Either one. Men in general, I guess. Didn't have a lot of nice to say about your brother, either."

She took a large mouthful of wine and scowled. "Stanley?" She shook her head. "I don't know about him. Smart as a whip. Killed it in school until Year 10. Then he started hanging out with some of Hanks' guys. Left school. Dealt drugs. Ran with a bad crowd. Mum was heartbroken. Dad wrote him off, but I think he hurt more than Mum did. He didn't show up at either of their funerals. Dad was really pissed off when he didn't show up for Mum's. Then he died a few years later, and Soph and I are still pissed at him for not showing up for Dad's funeral." She took another drink. "So I'm not surprised she was pissed off today."

The server arrived with our food. Steve and Gwen looked at my steak. Gwen shook her head a fraction and opened her mouth to say something. "Don't, Gwen. Let me enjoy without the criticism." I smiled at her and she picked at her salad.

"Actually, I was going to say I wish I'd ordered the same thing. Fuck diets."

I sliced the steak in half and dropped the smaller piece on Gwen's salad. "I could lose a kilo or two."

I watched her eat for a minute; so much like Sophie and so different. "You seem to be handling the Larry thing well. Better than I expected."

Steve looked at Gwen, then at me. "Who?"

Gwen topped up her glass and took a drink. "White doesn't go well with steak, but what the fuck." She looked at Steve. "Larry is the fuck who left me for his CFO. His CFO is twelve years older than me. I mean, she looks good for her age, but Jesus." She upended her glass and licked her lips. "I knew he was unfaithful, and I didn't do anything about it. Not that I know what I *could* have done about it.

"I'm in 'fuck it' mode right now. Next week I'll probably be bawling my eyes out, going through tubs of ice cream like cheese through a Frenchy." She fixed her stare on me. "So find my sister. I'm going to need help with the ice cream."

The bottle was almost empty, and Steve and I hadn't touched it.

"Steve, why don't you drive Gwen home? I'll follow and drive you back here."

"Thatsh not necessary."

"Oh, it sure as hell is." I nodded at Steve. He settled the bill, and I retrieved the keys from Gwen.

"You don't know where I live."

"Your car's navigation system has a 'Home' setting, right?" I walked with her out to the parking lot. "Your head is going to be ringing tomorrow."

"And the day after that, if I've got anything to say about it."

Steve met us in the parking lot and I handed him her keys. "'Home' in her nav system. I'll follow."

We got her home, made sure she locked up and headed back to the hotel. "So, what's on the schedule for tomorrow?"

"You're not up for continuing it tonight?"

Steve looked at me, and I laughed. "Fucking with you. We crash tonight, and tomorrow, without Gwen, we continue the canvassing. Soph left this car here, someone saw her walking."

"Maybe security video?"

"If we're lucky."

My phone vibrated in my pocket. I dug it out while navigating a corner. It was from a number I didn't recognise. I answered it and put it on speaker. "Mac Durridge. Who's this?"

"It's Cameron, Mac. Can you talk?"

"What's up, kid?" I handed the phone to Steve to hold.

"You wanted me to keep an eye on that phone, right?" I could hear a keyboard clicking in the background.

"It's late, Cam. Isn't it past your bedtime?"

"You want the help or not?" A couple of clicks. "Her phone bleeped this afternoon around 5:30."

"Up here in Kotara? Where. We'll head there now." I slowed and pulled to the curb, ready to go where Cam told me.

"Nope. A single location appears on Mandalong Road, just east of the M1."

"Heading to Morisset?"

"It's only one ping. It's on the correct side of

the road to be heading there."

I accelerated away from the curb. "Cam, I'm doubling your salary. Send me a screen shot and keep an eye on it. Call me as soon as something beeps, okay?"

I took the phone from Steve and hung up. "You might want to call the hotel and tell them we won't be staying," I said.

"Is it always this exciting?" He did something on his phone and put it back in his pocket.

"No. What did you just do?"

"Cancelled the reservation. They'll ding me a late cancellation change, but it's worth it." He grinned at me. "This is better than any show I've done."

I cocked an eyebrow and glanced sideways at him. "How old are you?" I didn't wait for an answer. "This is the 5% excitement. You lucked out. We're due the 95% of boredom, and it'll show up soon."

It was a frustrating drive. I could swing west and get on the M1, where 110 km/h would chew the trip up fast. But it would still take longer than the 80 km/h down the Pacific Highway. Felt like a fucking crawl.

Thirty minutes later we slowed at Dora Creek. Crossed over the bridge, train station on our left. I handed my phone to Steve. "Cameron sent the location. Guide me in."

He opened the phone and looked at the image. Looked at our surroundings and back at the phone. "Keep going. Through town and past the big traffic circle at Wyee Road. You know where the KFC is?"

I nodded. "Does it show?"

He laughed. "On Mandalong, just past that intersection."

I pulled onto the shoulder where he indicated and we got out. I looked across the street. "Over there, right?"

Steve looked at the picture on my phone, nodded and returned it to me. We looked both ways like good, careful people and crossed the road. There was nothing there but a Transport NSW depot, empty, gated and locked up.

"Fuck all to see here," said Steve.

"No shit." I made my way back across the wide road. "We're rapidly slipping into the 95%, mate."

"Okay. So what next?"

I looked at the time on my phone. "Back to base, get some sleep and start again tomorrow." I trotted across the last lane to avoid getting clipped by a ute. "She's back here, somehow, without her car. Full court press in the morning. Let's go."

"Come on, Mac. We're here. We keep going at it until we find her, right?"

I looked at him, tired. "We have no idea where she is. Her phone pinged here hours ago. She could be in Gosford by now. She could still be in Kotara and someone stole her phone. I'm tired. I won't be able to think through the problem without sleep. Get in the car. We're heading back to base."

Chapter Twenty-Two

They say the older you get, the less sleep you need. I don't know who 'they' are, but 'they' are full of shit. I walked and fed the pooch, hit the sack at 10:30, and slept until my phone rang at 7:04. I know that's what the time was because I tried to hit snooze, bleary-eyed, for about a minute until I realised it was a call.

"What?"

"Mac, you still sleeping? Breakfast at The Pelican. My treat." Jesus, but that actor arsehole could be chipper in the morning. He'd probably already gone for a jog, or spent an hour doing Pilates or some other bullshit.

"Yeah. Thirty minutes."

It was more like forty to walk and feed Linc, get my shit together, shower, and make it across the street. No shave. The thought of scraping a blade across my beat-to-shit face turned my stomach. When I arrived, Steve was well into a bowl of fruit, with a glass of fruit juice on the side. Christ.

I slid into the booth across from him. Jessie came over, happy for the excuse to be close to Steve. "Get me a couple of fried eggs, bacon, four slices of white toast and a gigantic fucking coffee, would you?"

Steve looked at his watch. "You're slow."

"And fuck you, too." I stretched my arms over my head. The shoulder blade wasn't hurting as much, but I could still feel a bit of a twinge. "We finish, we're heading to Morisset and walking the road. Seeing what video there is to grab from the businesses."

"It's still hot out there."

"We'll bring water with us."

Jessie placed a cup of coffee on the table, slopping some onto the table. "Who's in Morisset?"

I looked at Steve and shook my head. "A thing I got to do."

"What about what you're doing for me?" She looked back toward the kitchen, and I assumed her father. "You're still helping Alf, right?"

Ah, shit. "Look, Jess, something really urgent has come up that I need to attend to today. I'll be back at your case tomorrow, okay? This is serious. Sophie is missing."

She crossed her arms and opened her mouth a couple of times to say something, but I could see she was conflicted. Finally: "Is she okay?"

"Thanks for asking, Jess. We don't know. She didn't show up at her sister's place on Monday." I pointed at Steve. "We're getting close to tracking her down, I think."

"So get the police involved," said Jess.

"We tried. Last night. They weren't interested."

Steve reached across the table and tapped my arm. "It's day three, mate. Give it a try again."

I looked at the time on my phone and nodded. "Can't hurt." I scrolled to King's number and called.

"King speaking. Is this Mac?" She sounded too chipper for this early in the morning.

"Good morning, Lily. I want you all to

reconsider the Sophie thing. I need help. Your help."

There was a slight pause. "What Sophie thing?"

"I talked to Grange about it yesterday. He didn't mention it?"

"Mention what? What the hell are you talking about, Mac?"

I rubbed my hand over my face. Winced. I wouldn't do that again. "Sophie headed to Newcastle on Monday to visit her sister."

"Gwen?"

"Right. She didn't get there. Gwen showed up here yesterday asking for help. I called Grange, and he blew me off. Figuratively. We've got her phone pinging in Kotara a few blocks from where I found her car. And last night it pinged by the KFC in Morisset. So I'm pretty sure she was headed back here."

King tripped over her words. "Grange said nothing. I know Sophie well. This isn't like her. Get into the station as fast as you can. I'll be there in five. Give me the full rundown and we'll get some uniforms on it today."

A server placed my food in front of me, and my stomach responded with a grumble. "I'll be there in half an hour. Really appreciate it." I hung up and picked up a fork. "King will help."

Steve smiled. "I knew she would." He pointed at my plate. "All of that shit's going to kill you. You know that, right?"

I shoved a rasher of bacon into my mouth and chewed. "What exactly is the point of dying healthy?" I carved a large piece of fried egg and swallowed it without chewing. Yolk spilled, and I wiped it up with some toast and took a big bite. I was eating probably faster than I should, but I was hungry, and I had to get King up to speed.

I washed the food down with a mouthful of coffee. Finished what was on my plate in a few more mouthfuls and finished the java. I wiped my mouth with the back of my hand and burped. "Steve? Let's go."

I slid out of the booth and almost collided with Gerry. Jessie's father. Double shit.

"Gerry, good to see you. I'd love to stay and talk, but I've got to—"

"Jessie tells me you've stopped helping us, and you're off on some other case." His arms were crossed and he was flexing. I really didn't need this.

"This is short-term, Gerry." Hell, who is he to dictate what I do? "Listen, Sophie is missing. I need to head to the police station and update them with what we know. They'll be doing the leg work. I'll be back on Jessie's case before you know it."

He scowled, and I was afraid he was going to punch me. He's a big man. A punch would hurt. I put up my hands, semi-surrendering. "I know. It's serious. Jessie didn't do it, and the cops think she did, so the cops aren't our friends right now. But I need to get them looking for Sophie. I love her, and she's never gone missing like this before."

I love her. That's the first time I've ever said that. To anybody.

But it worked. He grunted and backed off half a step. "Go. Get back as fast as you can. I love Jess, and she's in very deep shit, right now."

"Fair enough. We'll be as fast as we can." I looked at Steve. "Ready?"

He nodded, I sidestepped Gerry and left The Pelican. Walked across the street to the parking lot behind my place where Steve had parked his car.

"Well, well, well. Mac and his movie star girlfriend." Dick Backney was leaning against Steve's car. Three of his muscle-bound friends were standing beside him.

Fuck.

Chapter Twenty-Three

I looked at Steve. "You going to run this time?"

"These are the guys, right?"

"Plus two."

Dick pushed himself off the car. "You boys just don't know when to back the fuck off."

I nodded. "Fair enough. I'm a little slow on the uptake. What in the hell are you talking about? Or do you even know?"

The three friends of Dick split off and took the other three points of the compass around us. I looked at Steve, and he turned to face the guy behind me. We were back-to-back. I hope he had a few tricks up his sleeves because this would get ugly.

I nodded at Dick. "You mute? What the fuck are you talking about?"

"Let the cops do what they gotta do, and that Jess girl goes away for a few years. Keep poking your nose in, and Jess gets hurt. And so does your girlfriend."

"Who, Steve? You called him my girlfriend before, but he's not gay."

"The bank girl. Back the fuck off. We let her go when Jess goes to jail. You keep poking your nose in, and we'll dump her out in the middle of the outback without any water."

I thought that's what he was talking about. I took a deep breath. Angry fighting would get me killed. "Hey, Steve-o, you up for a dance?"

He backed a half step, and our butts were touching. "As ready as I'll ever be. Is this part of the 95% or are we still in the five?"

"Still in the five, man. Stay strong."

I don't enjoy fighting. It rarely solves anything, and once you're past the age of about sixteen, the ultimate goal is killing the other party. Fighting that doesn't end in killing is a message left. Like yesterday. I still hurt from that one, but I had a sneaky suspicion today would be worse.

Dick rubbed his hands together like a man just told he was getting a favourite meal. Then he cracked his knuckles. Before he could swing at me, I hit him back first.

I stepped forward, clenched my right fist and pulled it close to my body. I twisted hard to the left, and my right elbow caught him on the side of the head. Much better than hitting a solid slab of bone with the small bones in your hand.

Dick's head snapped to his right, but his feet stayed planted. He was a fucking rock. I unwound my body and brought that same elbow back to the point of his chin. It rocked him back, but not as much as it should have.

He uncurled a haymaker aimed at the side of my head. I turned away from it and ducked behind my shoulder. He connected and staggered me sideways, and I stumbled on the gravel. I couldn't go down. He'd kick me to death. So I went with it, hit the ground on my shoulder and rolled back to my feet, bouncing like

Ali, warming up for the main event. I still hurt. The endorphins would have to carry me through.

From my new angle, back almost to the wall, I could see Steve in action. He had two guys flattened and was in the process of taking apart the third. It was fast, furious, and far more than I could manage.

The distraction cost me. Dick got within striking range before I had a chance to react. Stupid. I needed to focus. I swung at his face, and as he raised his arms to block it, I kicked him hard enough in the nuts to place 6 points from 80m. He doubled over, and when I moved in to finish him off, he lifted, his fist starting somewhere south of Hobart, intending an uppercut that would end me forever. I saw it coming. I couldn't pull back without landing on my ass. On the ground in range of his boots wasn't an option. So I moved forward, catching the blow in the stomach and falling forward on him.

I couldn't breathe. My diaphragm spasmed, but I was on top of him, and his nuts still hurt. Ruptured, I hope.

I looped my right arm around his neck as I fell. It was like a bull's neck. But the carotid arteries were close enough to the surface, just like with everyone else. I grabbed my left bicep with my right hand and put my left hand around the back of his neck.

And squeezed. Hard.

I fell on my back, and he landed on top of me, scrabbling at my arm. He telegraphed a back head butt. He moved his head forward a few inches, straining against my arm. I knew what was coming. I ducked my head to the right. He snapped his head back and would have broken my nose if I hadn't moved.

His head ended up beside mine. I whispered in his ear. "Feeling a little light-headed, Dick-o? Where's Sophie?"

It serves me right for being a smart-arse. He snapped his head to the right, catching my nose with the broad expanse of bone above his ear.

"Mother fuck!" I applied pressure even harder on the sides of his neck. He must have been fading. He struggled harder, so I grabbed his right ear with my teeth and bit, Tyson-style. He tried whipping his head away, blood flying everywhere.

My arms were tiring and the gravel was digging into my back, sharp stones cutting through my shirt.

He struggled, a bit weaker, and started kicking at my legs. Ineffective.

I arched my back and gave it one final squeeze. Everything I had left in my body.

We both released at the same time. Dick was out, and I had absolutely nothing left. I rolled him off my legs and pulled myself to my feet with the help of Steve's car. My head throbbed. Something was running down my nose, and I wiped it with the back of my wrist.

And almost blacked out from the pain. I slumped against his car and looked down at my shirt. It was covered in blood. I touched my nose and winced. The fucker broke it.

Steve didn't look much better. But he was standing. He shook out his hand and looked at the four bodies lying on the gravel. "I don't think I killed any of them. You?"

I laughed. "Dick is going to have a hell of a headache. And a nut sack the size of a cantaloupe. But he's not dead." I stepped closer and looked at the other three. "How did you do that?"

"Training, remember? Tons and tons of

training. Played a Navy Seal. The American accent was a bitch, but the six months of Krav Maga training I got more than made up for it. Intense, five hours a day, five days a week for six months." He smiled. "I need to send a case of scotch to the instructor. Paid off big time."

"So why in the fuck did you run off yesterday?" I kicked Dick in the head as I passed him. "These guys are useless. I shouldn't have hit them so hard. They could have told us something about where Sophie is."

Steve shook his head. "They wouldn't have talked. Too dumb."

"You're probably right. Get in the car. I need to get this nose checked out."

Steve eased himself into the driver's seat. He wasn't injury-free, but I wasn't going to ask.

"You didn't answer me. I got beat yesterday, and it looks like you could have handled them both yourself."

"I wasn't emotionally invested in the situation." He started the car and glanced at me. "Today I am."

He reversed out of the parking spot and left a

spray of gravel behind him. I looked over my shoulder. One of the three Steve had subdued was on his hands and knees, trying to stand. He copped a face full of gravel. At least he wasn't dead.

"Steve, buddy, you'll have bruises on a large percentage of your surface area. Your movie bosses aren't going to appreciate that."

He smiled, perfect white teeth gleaming in the sun. "Fuck 'em if they can't take a joke." He accelerated out of the parking lot. "Let's get your nose fixed up. This is fun."

Chapter Twenty-Four

Travel through triage at the hospital was a lot faster when you had blood all over the front of your shirt, and your nose pointed west when you were heading south.

I was ushered into treatment room 1.3. I think Steve got room 1.5. He didn't have as much blood, but his body was a palette of purples and blues.

I had almost given up on getting any treatment and was prepared to leave when the door finally opened, and Jane, the oldest intern in Australia, walked it. My day moved from shit pile to shit pile.

She entered with her head down, opening the folder holding my admission information. "So, Mr

Durr-" She stopped, a surprised look on her face, and looked over the folder at me. "Mac? Again? Are you trying to get here every day, now? I'm flattered."

"You betcha, doll-face. I got someone to break my nose just so I could get a chance to see you."

She threw the file on the examination bed and rubbed her left eye with the heel of her hand. "I've been here since six last night, and I'm really fucking tired. I'm going to splint your nose and you're going to leave me alone. Deal?"

"Deal." I held out my hand to shake on it and she ignored me. I waited for a minute, then let it drop in my lap. "So fix my nose already."

She got me to sit up on the examination bed and stood in front of me between my legs. She held my head in her hands, one on each side of my face. She leaned in close and looked at my misshaped nose, slowly moving my head back and forth to get better views.

"You're a mess."

I nodded. "That's right."

"There seems to be a lot more blood on you than you'd expect from a broken nose."

I looked down at my shirt. A lot of Dick's ear blood had pooled on me when I was on my back, and he was lying on top of me.

"It's the other guy."

"Is that right?"

"That's right."

She moved her hands to my nose, thumbs on either side and wrenched it to my left without any warning. The bitch. It brought tears to my eyes.

She stepped back, and I held my nose gently with both hands. "Holy shit. Did you *really* need to do that? Oh, mother love of God, that hurt." I gingerly touched my nose. It didn't hurt anywhere near as much as it did earlier.

She opened a drawer and removed an aluminium T-shaped device with a curved base to the 'T'. She opened another drawer and removed a new roll of white adhesive tape. "Sit still, or it'll hurt more than you've ever hurt before."

"I've been kicked in the nuts."

"Good for you." She settled the splint on my nose, the top of the T across my forehead, slightly above my eyebrows. Then she applied so much tape you'd think she was in Miss Permeter's kindergarten class.

I'm sure it was ugly, but the stability to my snout felt good. I tapped it. It muffled the pain, also. The flesh-coloured tape made it almost unnoticeable. "This is good, Jane. You must be getting lots of practice."

She got me to sign a Medicare form, and I returned to the waiting room. Steve appeared a few minutes after I got there. When he saw my face, he started laughing. "Oh, that's priceless."

"Thanks. What's your status?"

"Nothing broken, tonnes of bruises. I'll hurt for a few days, but the good doc says I'll be sweet. You look like something from Silence of the Lambs."

"We still need to talk to King." I walked to the car and held out my hand. "Let me drive this time." I wrestled my phone out of my pocket to call King.

I didn't get a chance to call her. She called me. "Mac, where are you?"

"I'm on my way there. Got side-tracked and ended up at the—"

"No shit, you got side-tracked. I'm at the

parking lot outside your place. Four guys in the hospital, one of them missing a large chunk of his ear. Blood all over the place. Witnesses have told me that you and your new friend did the damage, and I've got to say, you surprise me. You have always avoided a fight."

"When I could. The same fuckers attacked me yesterday. I'm getting a little tired of it." I tried changing the subject, sort of. "So, about Sophie."

"No. I need you to come down to the station and give me a statement about what happened here. Bring your new friend with you also."

No, no, no. This was something I didn't need. "The witnesses, they told you what happened, right?"

"The guy with the ear—or without an ear, to be precise—wants to file charges."

I laughed. "The arsehole was trying to kill me. He's lucky I didn't keep squeezing his neck. Another thirty seconds and he would have been dead." I took a breath. "So, you're not going to help?"

"I've got a crime scene to process. Call the station. There's bound to be someone there who will take your information. And wait for me when you get there. We need to talk."

I hung up. "Like I need this shit." I downshifted and hit the Pacific Highway.

"Easy on the wheels, mate. What's wrong?"

"Dick wants to nail me for biting off part of his ear." I smiled at Steve. "Tyson-like."

He turned sideways in his seat. Looked at me like I was crazy. "Those fuckers started it."

"And thanks to you, we ended it," I said. I slowed down and turned onto Wyee Road. "We're not going to go to the station. King will keep us tied up for hours giving her a story about that fight. It's over in five minutes and takes five hours to get through the re-telling." We passed the tiny Wyee train station and took the corner into Wyee proper. All three blocks of it. I turned right, heading north.

Steve had his head back, eyes closed, wind fucking up his perfect hair. He opened an eye. "Still the 5%?"

"We are about to well and truly enter the 95."

We passed the fertiliser plant, and Steve's eyes opened. "What in the hell?"

"Makes you appreciate a non-convertible,

right?"

He flipped me the bird. We continued north, Morisset Golf Club on the right. Hit the traffic circle at Mandalong Road and took the third exit, heading right toward Morisset. I pulled into the parking lot for the Morisset multi-purpose centre.

I turned off the ignition. "The last ping from Sophie's phone was about a hundred metres behind us. In front of us, for about a kilometre, are a couple of thousand people who might have seen something." I laughed at the look on his face. "No, we're not going to talk to all of them. But we're going to talk to as many as we can."

Chapter Twenty-Five

There was no point in splitting up at this point. Everything was on the north side of the road, at least until we got to the country club. We walked into the multi-purpose centre, and the staff didn't even see me. Steve was swarmed, like bees to clover.

I let them get their thrills for a few minutes before I broke up the crowd. "Steve, help me out here, okay?" Then louder. "People, we need your help." I held up my phone. A head and shoulders shot of Sophie smiling at the camera. "This is Sophie Patterson. She's been missing since Monday afternoon. The last time her phone registered with the network was yesterday, about a hundred metres west of here. We're hoping somebody may have seen her. Maybe she was walking, and her phone died around here." I slowly panned my phone so all of them could see the photo.

None of them showed any sign of recognition. I held it up long enough for them to take a good look, but nothing.

"Okay. Thanks for your time. We'll let you get back to what you were doing."

Steve went through a final round of selfies before I got him out of there.

"You have fans," I said.

He nodded. "This may be your 95%, but it's my 5%."

"How's that?"

"The months of preparation, the sixteen hours on location for five minutes of on-screen time, the days and days of ADR during post, that's my 95% work-work-work. The interaction with the people who enjoy what I do, who get that vicarious thrill of being in the presence of someone they've seen on television or streamed on their laptop, that's *my* 5%."

"Good. So you won't be bored. And it

entertains me just a tiny bit. But we still have a lot of people to talk to. You'll be fully sick and tired of your 5% by the end of the day."

We walked east on Mandalong, stopping at the small, home-run businesses and private homes along the north side of the road. We met with similar results: tonness of selfies and nothing to help me find Sophie.

"We're not getting anywhere, Mac."

"It's a slog."

"And Jess is closer to trial and we've got nothing to help *her* with."

I nodded. "I feel a slight twinge of guilt looking for Sophie and putting Jess on the back burner, but they're tied up, one and the same. We find Sophie, we get closer to what the fuck is going on." I looked ahead. Maccas. And a crowd.

"I think the selfies have gone online. There's a crowd gathering, and it's not for the Happy Meal."

Steve looked at the crowd milling in the parking lot of the fast food joint. "This isn't going to help us, is it?"

"Actually." I strode toward the crowd, Steve in my wake. "It might speed things up."

Someone in the melee spotted Steve. She sparked off a riot, with the crowd surging toward us. No, fuck that, surging toward Steve. They parted around me like I was a pebble in the Snowy River.

He handled them like a pro. Smiles and selfies. And as he finished with one, he'd direct them to me before he did the next one.

He got his selfies, but I got no joy. A few people recognised Sophie from the bank, but nobody had seen her in the past week.

The last visitor didn't ask for a selfie, but I imagined it took a lot of self-control.

"Senior Constable King. How ever did you find us?"

She chuckled. "You guys are firing up social media. Couldn't hide even if you tried." She gestured at a booth in the corner of the restaurant. "Have a seat, please. This won't take long."

"I'm getting some food first. You want anything?"

Steve and King were paragons of culinary virtue. I, on the other hand, was starving. I took my food back to the booth and found King and Steve in deep discussion—something about his childhood and his memories—and hers.

I slid into the seat and shook the fries out on my tray. Added three packets of tomato sauce. "Want some?"

"I want to live to a very old age, Mac. I'll pass, thanks," said Steve.

"Right." I slid the tray a fraction toward King. She looked at Steve, shrugged and grabbed a couple.

"You're corrupting her, Mac."

She patted her stomach. "Corruption started a long time ago." She winked at me and took another. "Tell about the mess behind your place."

Steve and I looked at each other. He subconsciously rubbed his ribs, and I touched my nose splint. Couldn't help it. "They were waiting for us." I leaned back in my seat. "Full credit to Steve. If he hadn't been there, I'd probably be dead."

"Why were they waiting for you?"

"Two of them jumped me yesterday, too. Dick Backney and three of his friends today told me to lay off the Jess investigation, or, and this is where it got really interesting, Sophie would get hurt. They told me they wouldn't release Sophie until Jess was permanently behind bars."

I leaned forward. "Does that sound like something you'd do if Jess were actually guilty? Force the case?" I crossed my arms. "Dick needs to be brought in and questioned."

She smiled. "You didn't manage to beat it out of him?"

"It was over too fast. By the time I was finished, he was in no shape to answer."

"That doesn't sound like the Dick I know," said King.

I shrugged. "Truly, I got lucky. And I'm sure there'll be comeback. Big comeback. But if you lock him up on the 'threatening me' thing, maybe I won't have to worry about it for a while."

I snagged the last fry and looked at the time on my phone. "If you'll excuse us, King, we must continue our quest for information, one citizen at a time. Legwork and persistence. Remember?"

"I can't stop you. I'll talk to Dick and his boys and see if I can corroborate your story."

"Good luck with that, King." I slid out of the

booth. "Come on. The Country Club is across the road."

"You think she would have gone there? Really?"

"You don't skip anything, Steve-o. Nothing."

Chapter Twenty-Six

We could have skipped the Country Club. We couldn't get in without buying a membership and once we got in there, those few who deigned to talk to us knew nothing useful.

We stood at the traffic circle in front of the clubhouse. We looked east. More of the same with little chance of success.

"We keeping on keeping on?" asked Steve.

"Absolutely."

My phone vibrated in my pocket. It was my office number. "Mac speaking. Who's this?"

"Gwen. Where are you?" She sounded

breathless. There was a tremor in her voice.

"What's going on?"

"You need to get back here as fast as you can. Your place. Fast, okay?"

I started trotting toward the car, Steve running along beside me asking questions that I ignored.

"We left you at your house," I said

"And when you didn't come back this morning, I came to you. Get here as fast as you can."

"Why? What's going on?"

"Your office or flat or whatever it is has been trashed."

"Have the police been called?"

She hesitated. "No. Not yet. Whoever did this left a message. You need to see it."

I tossed the keys to Steve and hopped in the passenger side. I held the phone to my chest. "My place, Steve. And snappy." I put the phone back up to my head. "What was the message?"

"No, you've got to see it. Hurry up, please."

There was still police tape behind my place, and much of the blood still stained the gravel in the parking lot. I tore the tape off, bundled it like old homework and threw it in the bin. I ran up the stairs, two at a time—my exercise for the month.

The door was ajar, and the hinges loosened. I shoved it open to a mess like I hadn't seen in years. Gwen was sitting at my desk, holding a DVD in her hand. She leapt to her feet when I came in. "Mac, watch this." She looked at my face. "What in the hell happened to your nose?"

"I slipped." My computer sat on my desk, untouched, despite the mess, the file cabinets tipped, the few half-dead plants uprooted, and chairs broken. I sat in the only unbroken chair, slid the DVD into the side of the computer and waited for the default program to launch and play it.

Steve sat on the corner of the desk to watch. Gwen paced.

The image shook at the beginning. It was a quick pan over the interior of a working garage, then focused on Sophie, sitting in a chair. A corrugated steel wall was behind her. Nothing identifiable was in the frame other than her.

She spoke with a clear, steady voice. "Mac, you

need to stop. Stop looking for me. Stop looking for something to clear Jess. Just stop, if you know what's good for you. And me. You can't win. You put a couple of them in the hospital, but there are more. Many more. It's bigger than you think it is. And you getting into the middle of it isn't going to stop it." She sighed. "I'm sorry. Tell Gwen I'm sorry, too. Just go away for a while and let things be, okay? It'll be over when it's over."

The video cut to black immediately after she finished talking.

We were silent for a minute. Steve spoke first. "Good looking lady. And, if you don't mind me saying, she didn't seem to be under much duress."

"Something's not right." I dragged the progress bar back to the beginning and slowly stepped though the video frame by frame. Most of it was blurred. I couldn't tell anything from it. I stepped through until Sophie was on the far right edge of the screen—just her hand. Stopped stepping through and pointed at the screen. "I shouldn't be surprised. That's Sally's place. I recognise that massive toolbox."

"They're pretty common in garages, Mac," said

Gwen.

I pressed keys and the image zoomed in. "It's blurry, but the name on the box. 'D Backney'. It's Sally's place."

I looked at Steve. "Stay here if you want. I've got to go."

"She really doesn't look like she wants you to butt in."

"I don't give a fuck. It's an act. There's no way she's gone underground like that on her own volition."

Steve stood. "I'll drive. I think this is going to be the 5% for real."

Gwen took my seat after I left it. "I'll wait here. Should I call the police?"

I retrieved my shoulder holster and handgun from the gun safe. "Hasn't helped us so far. Don't waste your time."

She said something back to me, but I was already gone.

We pulled to the curb in front of Sal's. The place looked closed down. The garage doors were closed, and the interior looked dark through the shop windows.

I peered in the small garage door windows. It was too dark to see. But that was where the video was made. I was positive. I walked to the shop's front door and tested it. It wasn't locked. Now, I wasn't born yesterday and hadn't walked into a trap in years. I took out my handgun and carefully pulled the door open.

Nobody in there. Just dust. I motioned for Steve to hold back, to wait for me. "Stay here until I say it's clear."

"No point, Mac."

I looked over my shoulder. Steve was standing with his hands half-raised, Dick behind him with a gun to Steve's head.

I pivoted and raised my gun and copped a crack across the back of my head with something heavy and metal. It didn't knock me out because I managed to roll with it a bit, and it only glanced off me. But it hurt like a son of a bitch and distracted me enough for someone to grab my gun from me.

I ended up on my ass on the dirty floor, one of Dick's friends pointing a gun at me. Pointing *my* gun at me. And Steve stood in front of me with a gun held to his head.

Dick looked like hell. Dried blood caked his shirt. He had a bandage wrapped around his head, and the blood had seeped through where his right ear was supposed to be. I subconsciously scraped my tongue on my teeth. "That looks painful, man."

I slowly stood, hands out to my side. Three more thugs types walked in. A skinny kid with a piss-poor attempt at a goatee laughed as he entered. "Right-o, Dick. You were right. He fell for it, hook, line, and sinker. Hook, line and *stinker*."

The kid paused for a second. Waiting for the applause, I guess. "What now?"

"They can meet our other guest." He reached into Steve's pocket and took his phone. "Check Mac for weapons.

The guy behind me jabbed me in the ribs and emptied my pockets. I have a really bad habit of talking when I should keep my mouth shut. He dug into my front pocket and got a little too close to my junk.

"You've got to buy me dinner and drinks before I let you do that, chum."

That got me a smack on the back of the head.

He herded me toward a door in the back of the shop. Dick was doing the same with Steve. When we got to the door, I was shoved through it. I tripped on the sill on the way in and landed on my face. Steve came in behind me, tripped over me, and I broke his fall. And one of the ribs that had just healed.

"Oh, fuck, Steve. Get off me." I rolled to one side and levered myself to the sitting position.

Sitting on the end of a sofa in front of me, a newspaper in hand and what looked like a cup of tea on a small table beside her, was Sophie.

She looked at me over the top of the paper. "Didn't I tell you to let this go? I meant it. You never listen. Fucking men."

Chapter Twenty-Seven

The door slammed behind us and it sounded like a bolt was slid into place. The room wasn't large, but it looked comfortable. In addition to the sofa were a couple of comfortable chairs, a TV on the wall and a fridge in the corner. Cozy for one. A little cramped for three.

I stood. Steve sat on the floor, looking a bit stunned.

"What in the hell is going on, Soph?" I asked.

She folded the paper and placed it on the sofa beside her. "Jesus, Mac. Why can't you leave well enough alone?"

"Are you part of this?"

"Oh, fuck no. I'm being held to keep you in

line. What a waste of time that turned out to be. Now we're all in here, and I have no idea what they will do with us. At least when it was just me in here, I was pretty sure they'd let me go when it was all finished."

I sat beside her. "Why were you pretty sure of that? When *what* is all finished? What have I walked into?"

She noticed who was sitting on the floor. "Is that Steve Ryan? Shit. How did you rope him into this?"

Steve stood and walked to the door and gave it a shake. "Five per cent, Mac?"

"Yup".

"Mac didn't rope me into anything. I wanted to ride along with him to get a feel for the life of a private investigator. Lucky me." He banged on the door, then moved under a window high on the wall and looked up at it. "I guess I got what I asked for." He turned and looked at Sophie. "I can see why he was hell-bent on finding you. You're stunning. A refined version of your sister."

She sat forward. "Gwen isn't with you, is she?"

I patted her leg. "No. But you're freaking her

the fuck out. You need to tell me what's going on."

"It's just like you think it is."

"No, I don't think so. You're here, comfortably stashed, while I'm running around the north coast looking for you. You could have called."

She looked at me for a second or two. "I'm being held, Mac. I just got here last night. I was held in a shit hole in Newcastle for a couple of days until my brother found out, then he got them to move me here." She looked at Steve, who was tapping the walls. "There's no way out, mate. These guys know what they're doing. I've already gone the round. It's impenetrable."

"I can vouch for that. Stormed the place a couple of times in my police days." I sat down beside her. We both sat sideways on the sofa, facing each other. I took her hands in mine. "What the fuck, Soph?"

"I know. I stopped in Kotara, and they were there. Picked me up right off the street. Took my phone and locked me in the back room of a food warehouse."

"Why?"

"You haven't figured it out yet? My brother ran with Monty, Davis and the crew."

"The surfer dudes? Baldy and Shaggy?"

"Them. The ones Jackson shot. You witnessed it. Jackson had to be punished. Jess is an unfortunate by-product. She'll get off lightly, with her young age and clean background. Stay out of it." She grimaced. "Actually, you don't have much of a choice now. You're right in it."

I was shocked. "You're okay with this? Jess is a kid. This will kill her. And her parents. I can't believe this."

"There's a lot about my family you don't know. Stan is the black sheep, but blood is thick." She got up from the sofa and paced the room. "Don't judge me, okay? It's the least of all possible bad scenarios."

I shook my head. I followed her across the room. "For some, maybe, but not for me. Do you think I'm going to put up with this? This is ridiculous. And you're crazy if you think they're just going to let us walk at the end of this."

"They will. I trust my brother."

Steve grunted. "You're nuts if you do. Sorry,

Mac, but she's nuts."

The door slammed open, and Dick walked in. Still bloody, still with a bandage wrapped around his head. The ink on his arms danced as he flexed his muscles.

He held my gun at waist level, pointing it at Sophie. "We're tired of this nonsense. Thanks for showing up, Mac. You made the job easier. Too bad you hang with him, Steve-o. There'll be tonnes of teen tears shed when your body washes up in a couple of years. Mac, one question: Are there any others who know we're involved?"

"King and Grange. We disappear, and they'll know it was you."

Dick laughed. "We've been dodging those idiots for years. I seriously doubt if anyone will care if you disappear off the face of the earth."

Sophie took a step forward and was stopped by Dick jabbing the gun in her direction.

"Stan said we'd be released," she said. "What are you talking about?" Her hands were trying to strangle each other.

Dick chuckled. "Your little brother is a pretty

convincing liar. Make your peace. I'll be back after dark."

He backed out of the door, pulled it shut and bolted it. I heard a padlock clatter against the metal door and Dick's steps receding.

I looked at Sophie. She was crying quietly. "Sorry, Soph. About your brother." I pressed my hands against the door. "We need to get out of here now, though. No time to fuck around."

"How are we going to do that, Mac?" asked Steve.

"You haven't had any training for a situation like this?" I smiled and looked at the hinges. "These guys may be tough, but they're as dumb as rocks." I looked around the small room. "I need a flathead screwdriver or a table knife. Something thin and flat."

Chapter Twenty-Eight

Thank God for stupid criminals. The door opened inward. The hinges were on the inside. "We need to pop the pins." I scanned the room, looking for anything strong and flat.

Steve pawed through the desk, pulling out the drawers and tipping them upside down. Sophie was doing her part, but there weren't many places to look. It was a small room. The search took not much longer than a few minutes.

"Nothing," I said.

"We could make noise and jump them when they come in," said Steve.

"Only in the movies. I don't think we'd be as

lucky this time. They know you've got some skills.

Steve thought for a second, then smiled. Unbuckled his belt, removed the buckle and handed it to me. "Will this do?"

I hefted it. "It's strong enough. Gonna fuck it up pretty bad, though."

"Whatever. Show me how you do this."

Sophie grabbed the buckle. "Do the bottom one first or it'll bind when you get to it." She jammed the edge of the buckle between the pin head and the hinge and twisted. The pin slid up a few millimetres. She pushed the buckle in a bit farther and then pushed down on the buckle. The pin pushed up a couple of centimetres.

"Good, Soph. Hang on a sec." I grabbed the head of the pin and pulled. It was still too tight. "Hand me the buckle for a second?"

"I got it," she said. She angled the buckle up so the edge was now placed under the head of the hinge pin. She clenched a fist and handballed it. Twice. The second one popped the hinge out and it clattered across the floor.

We stopped and listened to see if anyone else

heard it. But it was quiet.

I took the buckle from Sophie and attacked the middle hinge pin. The buckle was taking a hell of a beating. "I hope this isn't valuable."

"Don't worry about it. Get going."

A couple of hard taps and the pin popped out of the top of the hinge. Steve caught it before it hit the ground. I nodded in thanks and started on the top pin. The door sagged a tiny bit in the frame, binding the top pin in the hinge.

"Steve, hold the door up. Lift on the knob while I get this."

He grabbed and lifted. Sophie paced behind us. I'd have a talk with her later.

With the pressure off the pin, tapping it out was much easier. Three smacks on the underneath of the head, and the pin popped free. I caught it myself before it hit the ground.

Sophie looked at the door. "Now what?"

I jammed the buckle between the door and the jamb, just above the middle pin and pushed the exposed part of the buckle away from the door, levering the door out a few millimetres. Repeated the exercise up and down the door until about half the width of the door was pulled out on the hinge side. "Now, this."

Using the buckle as a lever, I placed one end under the part of the hinge still on the door, used the hinge on the frame as a fulcrum and pushed. The door moved far enough away from the frame to get a handhold. "Grab a piece, Steve."

I moved to make space for him, and we slowly pulled the door open from the hinge. The bolt, keeping the door locked, cracked the wood frame. When the door was about a meter open, I put my back against the frame and shoved. "That'll do. Sophie, follow me, Steve, take the back. If you see anyone, don't wait for an invitation, hit them as hard and as fast as you can."

"If I can avoid that, I am," said Steve.

The room was at the back of the garage. We had two options. Directly in front of us, across the hall, was a door into the shop part of the garage. Or we could turn right and go down the hallway into the garage proper. I was well and truly tired of this place, and going through the store was the fastest option, but that way held more of a chance of an audience. I turned right and made my way into the garage.

There were three cars parked in the two-bay garage. On the left, elevated on the hoist, was an aged ute, dozens of little dings and scrapes attesting to its life of work. It looked like it was half way through an exhaust replacement. On the right, two cars were nose to tail. An old Mercedes up front and a Toyota in the back, almost touching the rolling door. The closed rolling door. I looked in the window. The keys were in the ignition.

"Well, we've got wheels if we can open this."

"The place is empty." Steve pointed at the locked controls for the roller door. A keyhole at eye level with a lit red light and an unlit green light. "Do you think they'd keep the key for this on the premises anywhere?"

Sophie slumped against the Toyota. "They don't. It would be stupid to, wouldn't it? Someone could break in through the shop, find the key and empty the garage." She finger-combed her hair back. "This isn't going to end well, Mac. We should have just let it play out."

I didn't know her like I thought I did. "And

have Jessie spend the next decade or two behind bars for something that one of your friends did?"

She winced. I turned away before she could answer and swore. Steve moved to the back of the garage, looking for something.

"No hinge pins on this." I looked at the locking mechanism. "I might be able to figure out how to short the circuits of I can break this open." I looked back at Steve, who was doing something near one of the large toolboxes. "Can you bring me a large hammer?"

"Hang on a second, Mac. I think I can be a bit subtler than that." He returned to the door, holding up a couple of what looked like flat wire brush bristles. "I played a cat burglar in 'Diamonds Are a Man's Best Friend'. Shit movie, but I researched lock picking. This should only take a second."

It took almost five minutes, but when he was finished, the lock turned, the light turned green, and the door started rolling up—way too slowly.

"You're a handy guy to have around, Steve. Get in the Toyota, both of you. We've got to get out of here before someone picks up on the alarm," I said.

"I don't hear an alarm."

"It's silent," said Sophie. "Tied into their house. Someone will be here any minute."

Steve looked at us like we were crazy. "I just unlocked it. There shouldn't be any alarm."

"There is. Trust me." Sophie got in the front seat and I got behind the wheel. Steve crawled in the back, pushing fast food detritus out of the way. "Lovely set of wheels, Mac. Get back to where mine is. I don't think I can take too much of this."

I turned the key. It started almost immediately. I looked over my shoulder to back out. Dick was pulling up to the garage on his motorcycle. "Shit."

Chapter Twenty-Nine

Sophie and Steve both looked out the back window.

"What did I tell you, Mac," said Sophie.

Steve shook his head. "Too fast. And I unlocked the fucking thing. There is no alarm, silent or otherwise."

"Kind of a moot point now." I floored the accelerator and released the clutch. Handling was strange. I'd never lit rubber up in reverse before. The smoke from the rubber filled the car through the windows, and steering was like using a rudder to guide a tinny.

Dick managed to get most of the way out of

my path, but I glanced off his back wheel pretty hard. The car shuddered, and spittle sprayed from his mouth as he yelled something at me while he dove out of the way. I didn't stop to have a conversation. Cranked the wheel hard to the right, double-clutched, shifted into first and executed an almost perfect J-turn.

Sophie was hanging on to the dash and Steve had a grip on my headrest. I heard a few shots from behind me, but by the time Dick had fired at us, we were too far away for him to be a threat.

Sophie kept her neck craned, looking out the back window at the receding garage. "We're going to pay for that."

I yanked the wheel and slid to a stop on the gravel on the side of the road.

"What are you doing? He's going to catch up to us." Panic etched her face. She kept shifting her look from me to the window like she was expecting an army of bad to appear behind us.

"I fucked up his bike. If it was okay, he wouldn't have taken potshots at us. He would have righted his wheels and chased us. No way I'd be able to outrun him in this piece of shit, and he knows it."

"The others."

"Fuck that, for a minute. What in the hell is going on with you? Willing to let Jessie take the rap for Jackson's death? You? That's not a Sophie I know. And you seem to know these guys pretty well."

She turned and faced forward, occasional glances to the rearview mirror betraying her concern.

"Well?"

Steve leaned between the two seats and tapped on the console. "Maybe take this up with her later, mate? I'm not up for another fight."

I stared at Sophie's profile for a minute, then put the car in gear. I pulled off the shoulder as Sally sped by in her ute, a couple of her hard guys sitting beside her. I thought they missed us until they slid to a stop and executed a K-turn in the middle of the road.

"Fuck." I tromped on the accelerator and popped the clutch. I had to hand it to them. The old Toyota was running really well. Unlikely it would stay ahead of Sally's truck very long, though.

I jerked the steering wheel left, lightly hit the emergency brake and skidded off the Pacific Highway and onto the road to San Remo. I accelerated and took the next right and an almost immediate left, and pulled in front of a boat trailer and stopped. "Heads down."

I slid forward on my seat. Sophie leaned sideways and put her head on my lap. Steve had a lot more room than either of us and slid sideways below the window line.

"We're sitting fucking ducks," said Steve, muffled, from somewhere near the floor.

"There are half a dozen Toyota's on this street alone. They'll be looking for a moving car. Just sit still and shut up."

Sophie looked up at me. "Stan told me that this was just temporary and that Jess wouldn't have to spend any time in jail. Diminished capacity or something."

I shook my head and slowly eased up to see the side mirror. Nothing behind us. Yet. "You believed him? You and Gwen have done nothing but bad mouth him every time you talk about him, and you pick this time to believe him?"

Sal's truck turned onto the street we were on and raced past us. I closed my eyes, some primitive part of my brain convincing me that if I couldn't see them, they couldn't see me. Jesus. I was fantastic in a pinch.

I opened my eyes after the truck dopplered past us. They slowed at the next intersection and then turned right in a cloud of tyre smoke.

Sophie's head popped up. "They're gone?"

I pushed it back down. "Not yet."

We sat there for another five silent minutes. After the rumble of her V-8 and the squeal of tyres had faded, and there had been silence for at least a minute, I sat up. "We should be good."

"They'll be looking for us." Sophie looked around, a meerkat in a Toyota.

"No shit."

I started the car and pulled from the curb.

"It might be a trap. They're probably waiting for us somewhere."

"Unlikely." Not as unlikely as I'd like. "I'll go out the back way, though, just in case."

I slowly drove through San Remo until I reached the Central Coast Highway—no contact with the bad guys.

"We can't go back home."

"No," I said. "But I know a place you can hang

247

at for a little while. I know someone who could use some visitors."

Chapter Thirty

I drove north on the Central Coast Highway until it turned into Wyee Road. I followed it past the small train station, through the town and to a large house hidden behind a stand of trees just south of the fertiliser plant.

I pulled into the driveway, past a black Lexus and a beat-up Ford SUV, and cut across the broad expanse of lawn. I pulled the car around to the back of the house. Betty was sitting on the deck, under cover, a book in her lap and an icy drink by her side. She watched as we climbed out of the car and walked toward her.

The terra cotta deck was as large as my

apartment. A six-burner barbecue sat in a small alcove, looking like it hadn't been fired up in years. Hanging plants provided a light screen around the glass-topped table, giving the place a cosy feel. A wicker lounge chair sat beside an upright chair, a table between them.

Betty took a sip of her drink, placed it on a coaster on the small table and stood as we approached. "You're ruining the lawn." She looked at my nose. "You're not looking any better."

"Betty, you know Sophie. And this is Steve Ryan."

"Why are you here, Mac? I told you I wanted some time alone. Mostly from Ernie. He's a philanderer."

Sophie stood back, her hands clasped in front of her. "Mac has known where you've been all along?"

A small smile flitted across Betty's face. "He has. He owed me."

"Don't worry, Betty. You paid for solitude; you've got it."

Steve turned his back to us and looked out over the broad expanse of lawn. "It must cost a fortune to keep this looking like this."

"I have tank water and a ride-on mower." Betty smiled. "That's actually quite fun." The smile slipped from her face. "Why are you here?"

"We seem to have pissed off Sally and her crew. I'd like Sophie to stay here with you, if that's okay, until it dies down."

The look from Sophie would curdle milk. "I don't need your protection." She walked back toward the car. "So fuck you."

I ran after her and took her by the arm. "You heard them. They talked about getting rid of us. Killing us and disposing of our bodies. One of them killed Jackson, an ex-cop. They'd have no hesitation about killing all of us."

"And you're dragging Betty into this?"

"Nobody knows she's here. There's at least another three weeks' worth of food in her pantry, and she could use the company. Do it for me. These guys are animals."

She clenched her jaw muscles and thought about something for a minute, then visibly relaxed. "Okay. But only if it's okay with Betty."

We walked back to the deck, to Steve listing the

various movies he'd been in. Betty claimed to have not heard of any of them.

"This has been a truly humbling experience, Betty. I'm going to send you some DVDs."

"I only watch the news and documentaries. If you're in the news or narrating a documentary, send me one of those." She switched her focus to me. "Have you and the princess decided what you're doing?"

Jesus, it was never easy. "Yes. Please let Sophie stay here for a couple of days. It won't be any longer than that."

Betty looked at Sophie, head to toe, for a full minute before speaking.

"You work at the bank, right?"

Sophie nodded.

"Do you smoke?"

"Haven't in years. Look, if this is going to put you out, I can go to my sister's place in Newcastle."

Betty raised her eyebrows and looked at me. An unspoken question that I read loud and clear.

"No, that's how all of this started. If you don't stay here, I will have to drive you into Sydney and put you up in a hotel. That's four hours of travel I'd rather spend on closing this down."

Betty acquiesced. "Okay. I guess a conversation or two in the evening wouldn't hurt. Where's your luggage?"

"I don't have any. This was spur of the moment," said Sophie.

"And we can't return to my place to get her clothes. That'll be one of the places they're looking," I said.

"Oh. You're living with him?"

Sophie looked at me. "For now."

I looked at my watch. "Steve and I have to run. Sophie, Betty, if you need anything, call me."

Sophie didn't even move toward me for a hug or kiss or anything. And I thought *I* was having reservations.

Steve waited until he got into the car before he talked again. "She had absolutely no idea who I was."

"Don't bet on it. She's a joyless harridan."

"You speak of all your customers that way?"

"Only the really rich ones. Her father owns a couple of the coal mines around here."

I started the car and tossed a small unanswered

wave at Sophie and Betty, then turned around and drove out the way we came in.

"You're really concerned about Sophie, aren't you?"

I looked at him. The bruises on his jaw were stunning, and the swelling on his lip was ripe. "I am."

"Because she might be in danger? Aren't we all in danger?"

"I think you and I might be in more danger than she is." I didn't want to say it out loud, but it was undeniable. "She was too willing to let Jessie fry for this. And didn't she seem to be a bit too relaxed when she was being held in the garage?"

"You think she's part of it?"

I ease out of the driveway onto Wyee Road. "I hope not. It looks like it, though. Betty will keep an eye on her, and she'll call if Sophie leaves."

Steve nodded. "Fine. So what now?"

"Back to pick up Cameron. We need another set of fists."

"But you just told Betty that we couldn't return to your place because that'll be one of the first places they look."

"You can't run away from your problems, Kid. Face them head-on. Take whatever they throw at you. Defeat them."

Chapter Thirty-One

"Can we get back to my car?" Steve adjusted himself in the seat. The car was old, the dash was faded and there was a funny smell that seemed baked into the vinyl seats.

"You don't like my stolen car?" I smiled at him. "Do I have to remind you where you parked? You really want to head back to Sal's place?"

He stared out the window and tapped on the glass with his knuckle. "Maybe not yet." He looked at me. "But we can't put it off forever."

"No, we can't. But we have something to do first."

There were some people who needed to know what was going on. Jess was on the receiving end of a bogan conspiracy. Why her, I hadn't figured out yet. But she needed to know, her parents needed to know, and Alf needed to know.

"So are you going to tell the cops what's going on?"

Oh, yeah. Them too. I dug my phone out of my pocket while I negotiated the traffic circle onto Ruttleys Road. I handed it to Steve. "Find Grange in here and give him a call. Put it on speaker."

"Password?"

I told him. He fumbled through the menu, cursing under his breath. Technology had certainly improved since I got that phone. He apparently found it because I heard a ringtone from the far end of the call. He held the phone between us. Grange answered after a few rings.

"What do you want, Mac? I'm busy."

"You're on speaker with Steve Ryan."

"Who?"

"It doesn't matter. Look, this is about Jackson's murder." We crossed the bridge over the train tracks. The express into Hornsby passed under us, just leaving Morisset train station. "Jess didn't do it."

"Talk to her lawyer."

"I was just held against my will in Sal's garage. I was told that I'd been sticking my nose in too much and that I should back off and let Jess take the rap. Have you looked at Sal's mob?"

There was background noise in the police station, and I missed the first of his response, but it ended with "—bullshit."

"Didn't catch that, Willy."

"Detective Sergeant Grange, to you. It's bullshit, Mac. The evidence is clear. And it's not my job now anyway. It's with the courts. I'm busy, Mac. Stop tilting at windmills."

The call dropped. Which is to say the fucker hung up.

Steve handed the phone back to me. "That went well."

"He's busy. And he's right. It's with the courts. I need to talk to Alf."

It was a twenty-minute drive to The Pelican. I

got Steve to call Alf and ask him to meet us there.

When we pulled into the parking lot, the sun was getting close to the horizon. The heat had eased, and a cool breeze came in off the bay. It was a nice change. The temperature was down around the low thirties, and it felt chilly.

Alf, Jess and her parents were sitting at one of the large tables, waiting for me. Sue slid a cup of coffee across the table as I sat—nothing for Steve.

"What's this big news, Mac?" asked Alf. "And why couldn't you just tell me on the phone?"

I took a drink of coffee. I probably wouldn't sleep tonight anyway. And I was starving. "Can we get some food? I'm working up an appetite."

I was past the point of caring. My stomach thought my throat was cut. I looked at them until Gerry shook his head and walked back to the kitchen. He said something to someone and came back to the table.

I clasped my hands together on the table. "Okay. Good. Sophie, Steve and I have been held against our will by the people who killed Jackson." I held up my hands and stopped the inevitable barrage of questions. I could see the questions on their faces. "We broke out and pissed off, and they'll find me eventually. If I don't find them first." I looked at Gerry. "Help would be nice. The more bodies, the better." I placed my hands flat on the table. "They are framing Jess. I can't prove it yet, but Alf, you've got to look at that angle. Try digging something up. There has to be a link between Jackson and Sal's guys." I stood. "I was serious, Gerry. I'm heading back. Steve is coming with me. I'm going to draft Cameron. He's a big lad and should come in handy. I'll beat the truth out of them if it kills me. You in?"

A large pizza appeared on the table. I took the first slice and gingerly took a bite, burning my lips on the cheese. "And we need to find Jess's kite bag. Someone's prints will be on it. Dick's or Harry's or someone else, not Jess."

Steve took the second slice, surprising all of us. "What? It's a cheat day." He rolled his shoulders. "And if we're getting into it again with these guys, I need all the fuel I can get."

The pizza was good. I scarfed down another

slice and stood. "Okay. On to it."

Gerry stood and put his hand on his wife's shoulder. "Don't say anything, Suzie. I'm going, too."

He could catch up. I was out the door and halfway across the street before he left. I took the stairs two at a time. Cameron jerked his head up when I stormed through the door. Lincoln almost took my feet out from under me and I ended up accidentally kicking him.

"Shit, Mac. You scared the crap out of me. What's the rush? I was heading home."

I gave Lincoln a reassuring pat. "Where's Gwen?"

"She got a phone call about fifteen minutes ago, then pissed off. Didn't even say goodbye."

I had an idea I knew where she went. "Want to make an extra couple hundred bucks?"

Steve pushed in front of me. "He's just a kid, Mac. Don't."

Cameron did that peacock thing. He pulled his shoulders back and stuck out his chest. Flexed every muscle in his body. "What's up, Mac? I can handle it."

"I know you can, kid. We need to bust some

heads that have been fucking with us. You game?"

"Hell yeah. Who?"

"Sal and her minions."

Cameron backed up a couple of steps, then sat. Slowly. "Oh." He swallowed and rubbed his arm. "Really?"

"Really." I shrugged. "Could use the assist, but if you're not up to it..." I let the sentence hang. People have called me a dick in the past. Sometimes, they're right.

"Yeah, well," he swallowed. "Look, I can go with. Not sure how useful I'll be."

"That's the ticket. You'll be fantastic. Look at yourself. Playing rep level footie, strong as an ox. Fast, agile, and a fucking bull, if you don't mind me saying." I nodded toward the door. "Gotta go now. This has to end tonight. One way or another."

"One way or - what exactly do you mean by that?"

"Those motherfuckers are going to regret ever having fucked with me and mine. And I really appreciate your help." Headed for the door.

"We're going to die."

I stopped and looked at Cameron. Massive, rangy, young. Probably not a single ache or creak in his bones. "We all die. Better to die doing heroic endeavours than to whimper into the shadows."

"Shadows can be good."

I laughed. "Come on, Cam. It'll be an adventure." I nodded toward the door. "Trust me."

Steve frowned at me. Cameron headed through the door in front of us, and Steve grabbed my arm and stopped me from following him. "Don't bring him along. He really is going to get killed."

"We need the manpower. And Alf is too old to be any use."

"You're a dick."

I nodded. "Hurry. We're losing light."

Chapter Thirty-Two

The door slammed shut behind me, and Steve caught up halfway down the stairs. "Mac. Mac, no. I'm not going with you if you insist on taking the kid along."

"Really? He's got ten kilos on you, is as fit or fitter than you and we need all the help we can get."

"And the last fight he had was on the field. He's useless when the other guy actually wants to kill you. He'll be stomped to death in minutes."

I looked down the stairs. Cameron was leaning against the car, hands in his pockets, head down. Screaming 'target'. I'd seen him play. Hell of a ruckman. Tough as nails on the playing field. Down there by the car, he looked scared shitless.

"Okay. You're right. You and me and Gerry aren't going to be enough, though. As good as you were before. I have a feeling they'll be ready for us this time."

"Round up some of your friends."

I walked down the stairs. I got to the bottom and called Cameron over. "Take off, kid. Go home. Thanks for the help looking for Betty. That's all finished. If I need a computer hack job, I'll call you." I slapped him on the shoulder. "You've been great. Scram."

"What about the—"

"I've got it. We've got it. You're right. You'd be slaughtered."

"Call the cops. You don't have to do this."

"Tried that already. Look, I'm sure the police will help eventually. I'll get them across the line. But these arseholes threatened to kill me, and I'm not going to wait around for them to deliver on that promise." I watched Gerry cross the street from The Pelican. "We'll be fine."

Baz was sitting a bit down the sidewalk. He got to his feet and shuffled in my direction. "What's the deal, Mac?"

"Nothing, Baz. Go back to sleep." I turned my back to him and got in the car.

"Fuck off, Mac. Where's Sophie? They still got her?"

Well, that got my attention. "What do you know, Baz?"

He leaned into my window, the stink of stale sweat watering my eyes. "They still got Sophie? They got her at Sal's place. You know that, right?"

"How in the fuck? How did you know that?"

"I hear everything in this fucking town. If you're going to rescue Sophie, I'm going with you."

"I got her out. We got her out. Appreciate the thought, but we don't need your help."

"So you're going back to clean those fuckers up? I still want to go."

The last thing I needed. An alcohol-soaked homeless dude coated with the stench of a wombat's ass. "Stay here, Baz. Don't want you to get hurt."

He fucking sucker-punched me. His right fist snapped out like the end of a whip and caught me square on the jaw. "Don't fucking underestimate me,

Mac. You get tough living on the street." He wrenched the back door open and got in behind me and beside Gerry. "Where's pretty boy? Let's get going."

Steve leaned in the front window, looked at Baz and raised his eyebrows at me. "Really?"

"Get in."

We rode with the windows open. Baz kind of mandated it. The sun had disappeared, and the heat had gone with it. The crosswind through the open windows made discussion difficult. We mainly sat in silence.

As we approached the garage, Gerry placed a hand on the back of my seat and leaned through the gap. "So what are we doing here?"

Fine time to ask. "We're picking up Steve's car. Much nicer than this one."

Steve chimed in. "Not the best neighbourhood. Can't see myself leaving the car on the street overnight."

Gerry sat back in his seat. "Right." He leaned forward again. "What are the odds that there'll be a brawl?"

Baz took this one. "Ger, these fuckers framed your daughter for murder. I'll be seriously disappointed in you if there *isn't* a brawl."

He was homeless, not stupid. I pulled the car into the parking lot alongside Steve's convertible. We got out, hyper-aware. There appeared to be nobody there.

Steve took out his keys and pressed the fob, unlocking the car. "So, I'm just going to take this now." He eased into the front seat and looked around. Shrugged, put the key in the ignition and turned.

The front door flew open just as the car started. Dick and four of his friends streamed out. They arranged themselves in a semicircle around us, our backs to the fairly busy road. Dick was directly in front of me, in work pants and a singlet, looking pissed off and jacked a bit more than usual. The bruising on his neck obscured a tattoo, but the ones on his arms and shoulders were wriggling as he flexed. He still had a bandage on his ear, and I suspect it would be there for a long time.

Two friends placed on each side of him, all four looking like they aspired to be as big and ugly as Dick.

They tightened the half-circle a couple of steps.

Dick looked at each of us in turn, then looked back at me. He bunched his fists. Muscle and sinew rippled up his arms. "Mac. You came back. And they said you were the smart one." He nodded toward the garage. "You and your friends get your arses in there before we rip your arms off and shove them up your fucking arses."

Baz let out a deep, throat-shredding yell and launched himself at the guy on the far left of us. Hit him before the muscle head had a chance to react, flattening him and landing hard on his chest. He drove his elbow into the guy's throat and rolled off, jumping to his feet. Dick's friend rolled to his side, holding one hand to his throat, trying to breathe.

Dick was turned away from me, watching the Baz encounter—a perfect opportunity. I had to get him down to kicking level because there was no way I'd drop him with my fists. I drove my heel into the side of his knee. I heard something snap.

I'm too confident in my abilities. Before I had a chance to follow up with a knee to his head, he drove his fist at my groin. I saw it coming and pivoted. He caught the inside of my left thigh with a powerful blow, causing the muscle to spasm, dropping me to the ground. I made sure I landed on my left side and rolled. Baz was on the receiving end of a beating, and Gerry and Steve were in full battle.

I hobbled to my feet and faced Dick. He balanced on one foot. "Jesus, Mac. You're fucking stubborn."

"Why Jess?" I limped back as he hobbled toward me, not looking too happy. "She's just a kid. I know you or one of your friends killed Jackson. Retribution for Jackson killing those two surfer arseholes."

"It wasn't one of them." He jabbed himself in the chest with his forefinger. "Me. I did it. That fuck should have known better. You don't fuck with the family."

He lunged at me. His bum knee slowed him, and I got behind him on the garage side. Baz was out, curled on the pavement beside a dumpster. One of Dick's guys was out on his back, courtesy of Baz, and Steve had two of the others tied up in a massive battle. Gerry was putting the boot into a fourth, leaving me alone with Dick.

I was backing into the wall. The garage door was closed, but there was scrap on the ground outside, including a metre-long chunk of rusty exhaust pipe. I grabbed it and jabbed it at him. He danced back, putting weight on his recently damaged knee. He groaned and shifted onto his good leg.

"Dick-o, let's stop this. You're almost finished. Tell Grange it was you and get Jess off the hook."

Dick tipped his head back and laughed. "Not even close to finished. You're old. I'll finish you off and my friends and I will finish the rest of you."

Dick looked at Steve keeping two opponents at bay and I took that opportunity. I swung like I was going for a six at the MCG. Caught him in the forehead as he turned back. Snapped his head back and straightened him out like a cracked whip.

"Fuck. That was nice."

I spun around, ready to swing, and almost clocked Sophie.

Chapter Thirty-Three

I pulled the swing and almost dislocated a shoulder. Sophie stood there with her hands on her hips.

"When did you get here?" I asked.

"About ten minutes before you did. Straight from Betty's. She left the keys in her truck." She pushed me out of the way of a swinging pipe and kicked the guy swinging in the nuts. I drove my elbow into his jaw and knocked him stupid.

I followed through with *my* pipe and cleaned the legs from under one of the two Steve was working on. I kicked him in the head when he hit the ground. Steve was perfectly fine one-on-one, so I stepped in to help Gerry. I had no fucks left to give. Do or die, but preferable without the 'die' part.

It didn't take long after that. Surprisingly, we didn't suffer that many injuries. I think my left hand was broken. Baz had a couple of cracked ribs and a concussion, but he was making as much sense as he usually did. Steve was unruffled, the shit, and Gerry was nursing a sore shoulder but wouldn't elaborate on how much it hurt or what actually happened. Sophie was unscathed, but all she'd done was kick one of them in the nuts. Granted, it was a mighty kick.

Gerry pulled me to one side. "What did this accomplish, other than being massively cathartic?"

I dug my phone out of my pocket. "It may be as old as the hills, but it records. And I've got Dick on tape admitting to killing Jackson." I looked at the unconscious five thugs spread out at the entrance to the garage. "They'll keep. We get this to Grange or King and it'll be over for Jess."

"So he killed Jackson because Jackson killed a couple of his boys?"

"Yeah." I pointed at a couple of them. "See the small blue ringed octopus on their shoulders? They're in the same group. In for life."

Something twigged in the back of my brain. Something my brain was insisting was important, but it was being a bitch and not telling me exactly what it was. I couldn't force it. "Let's get going."

Baz headed toward Steve's convertible.

Steve got between Baz and his convertible. "Oh, hell no. He's not getting in my car. Gerry, hop in. Mac, smelly dude can go with you."

"The name's Barry, pretty boy. Baz to my friends, Barry to you." He smiled at Sophie. "You can come with us. Only room for two in Pretty Boy's toy."

Sophie jumped in the front seat. "Let's get the fuck out of here before reinforcements show up."

I got behind the wheel, and Baz crawled in and spread himself across the back seat. "Home, James."

Sophie covered her mouth with her hand. "Oh, Jesus. Open all the windows, Mac."

I looked over my shoulder at the man in the back. "Yeah, he's kinda ripe." I hit the buttons and lowered them all. It would make conversation difficult, but I felt like yelling anyway. Now I had an excuse.

I pulled onto the main road back in to town and pushed the piece of shit Corolla as hard as I could.

The wind roared through the windows. I looked over at Sophie. I had to yell to be heard, and really, I just had to yell. "What the fuck? How are you still showing up at these guys' place? Jesus."

She held the hair back out of her eyes. Looked out the windscreen for a minute before looking at me. "You sound like I'm one of their biker chicks. My brother is friends with them. That's it. Bad choices by my baby brother sometimes come back on me." She looked back out the front window. Set her jaw like that was that.

I wasn't finished. "Did you really go to Gwen's place, or was that a story? Were they really holding you?" I was yelling louder than the wind noise called for.

She snapped back to me. "Oh, Jesus, Mac. Yes, I was visiting Gwen. That was the intention. I never got there. I saw my brother's friends on the street, and they 'invited' me to go with them." She used her fingers to make inverted commas. "I didn't have a choice. So yes. They *really* were holding me. Fuck, Mac. You think I'm part of this?"

She crossed her arms and looked forward, hair

whipping around her face like a pissed-off Medusa. I had to ask, though. Too much wasn't making sense.

"But you keep showing up with them." I don't know when to shut up.

Baz leaned between the seats. "Shut up, Mac."

She kept her arms crossed and stared straight forward out the windscreen. Arms firmly and definitely crossed. "He's my brother. Most of them were school friends. They hung around with the wrong older crowd. Easily influenced." She clenched her jaw. "He's my brother."

Baz leaned forward. "Family, man."

"What older crowd?"

"What?"

I looked at her, then pulled over. "What older crowd influenced them?"

"What does it matter?" Sophie turned sideways in the seat and frowned at me. "It doesn't matter. It's too late. They are too far gone."

She turned away and covered her face with her hands. Her shoulders shook. Fuck. I placed a hand on her leg. "Sorry, Sophie. I pushed too hard. This is important, though. Who influenced them?"

She sniffed and wiped her eyes with the heels of her hands. "Jackson. And Sally's old man, whatever his name is. Hank."

I shook my head. "Jackson couldn't have had that much influence if they killed him."

"He was up there in the organisation. Under the radar while he was on the force. Corruption in the police department kept them going. Kept them from getting shut down."

The penny dropped. Oh, fuck. "We've got to get you out of here." I pulled from the curb in a cloud of exhaust. "And don't give me any of your 'I'm just as tough as you' bullshit."

She had a puzzled look on her face. "What do you know that I don't?"

"Who the other person in the force is. And he's going to want to shut down loose ends. You're a loose end."

Chapter Thirty-Four

I diverted to Betty's place. It was a bit of a bolthole for Betty and under everybody's radar. The house was in her mother's maiden name, and it was unlikely that anyone else knew about it.

"Who?" Sophie had a laser focus on me.

I glanced at her and focused on Ruttleys Road. It was a death trap with a single lane in each direction, especially with the sun on its way down. "Grange."

"Bullshit."

Baz leaned forward. "You sure about that? Would be pretty bad if you're wrong."

My phone vibrated, and I answered on speaker. "Mac here."

"Where you going?" asked Gerry.

"Dropping Sophie off at a safe place. Get back to The Pelican and get inside. Don't let anyone in. Shut the place down and go to ground."

"You think Sally will send someone after us?"

I thought about that for a minute.

"Mac? You still there?"

"Yeah. Possibly, she will. But possibly she has nothing to do with this. Just stay safe. You're on speaker?"

"We are," said Steve.

"Stay there with Gerry and family, Steve. I'll call you later. I need to check a couple of things out first."

I dropped the call just as I hit the traffic circle where Ruttleys Road met Wyee Road and turned left, then right, across traffic, into Betty's drive.

"She's annoying as hell, Mac."

"And so far under the radar, you should be good for the next twelve hours."

"What happens after that?"

"It's finished, one way or another."

She stared out the window at the house. I

stopped by the front door, and Betty stepped out.

"You're back."

Sophie stepped out of the car. "I am."

"Where's my truck?"

"At Sally's Smash Repair."

"You wrecked it?"

Sophie shook her head and walked toward Betty. "It's fine. Mac gave me a ride because we needed to get out of there quickly. There was a bit of an altercation."

Betty cracked one of the few small smiles I've ever seen on her face. "We'll go pick it up tomorrow. You come on in and tell me what went on."

The two women entered the house, and Baz jumped into the front seat.

"What now, Mac?"

I reversed in a tight half-circle and pulled out of the drive, stopping at the road trying to figure out my next steps.

"I've got to get Dick's confession to the police."

"Ya might wanna back it up, somehow."

Homeless, not an idiot. I selected the audio file

and sent it to Steve's phone. "Thanks, Baz." I called King.

She answered on the half-ring. "Mac, I'm on my way home. I waited for you to come in and you didn't. I'm going to have to put out a warrant for you tomorrow. Show up by 9, okay? I don't want to do the paperwork."

"Good evening to you, too. I just had another altercation with Sal's mutts. There's a mess at her garage. This time, though, I managed to get Dick admitting that *he* killed Jackson because Jackson killed the two surfer guys."

The call went silent. I checked the display to see if I'd dropped. I hadn't.

I stuck the phone back up to my head. "You still there, King?"

"Yeah. That changes things a bit. You'll testify to that?"

"I will. Don't have to, though. I've got it recorded." I pulled out of the drive and headed back to town. "Can I meet you at the station?"

She sighed. "I can get back there, but it'll be in about an hour. Grange is still there, though. I'll give him a call and tell him you're on your way."

No. Fuck. "Don't. No." I looked at the phone, and she'd hung up. I pressed redial, and the call immediately went to voice mail.

"Shit, shit, shit." I floored it around the traffic circle and hit Ruttleys at speed. Excessive speed.

"You're gonna fuckin' kill us, Mac. What the hell?"

"King is calling Grange to let him know we're coming in."

Baz had both hands firmly on the 'holy-shit-we're-going-to-roll' handle above the door. "That's a problem."

I crested the bridge over the tracks, and I think the Toyota I stole caught air.

"Jesus Christ, Mac. Getting us killed isn't going to help anyone."

Good point. I eased off a smidge, thanking the fact that traffic was light. I was all over the road, and there wasn't enough road. "Grange will make a beeline to The Pelican and grab Jess again. I need to get there first."

"I got that."

I slowed for a hard right bend in the road, accelerated out of it, and screamed past a speed trap. "Shit, shit, shit."

Red and blue lights lit up, and the siren shredded the night. Baz twisted in his seat. "This might not be a bad thing. Explain what's happenin' and get him to escort you."

I don't know about that. "This isn't my car." I pulled onto the thin shoulder. The cop car pulled in behind me. I dug my wallet out and rolled down my window. I watched in the side mirror as the young uniform approached with a torch in one hand and the other hand on his holster.

I recognised him. He came alongside the car and shined the light in the window, then played it across the back seat. His name tag said Warburton. This was the guy who took me to the station from the hospital.

"Small world, Constable."

He aimed the torch at my face. I held the gaze until I couldn't and looked away. "Well, Mac. This is going to save me a lot of time."

"How's that?"

He unclipped the holster and pulled out his sidearm. "How about the both of you slowly hop out of that stolen car and come around to the back."

Baz shrugged. "I'll get my three squares, anyway." He opened the door and stepped out. He bent down for reasons I'll never understand, just as Warburton pulled the trigger, missing him completely.

"Oh, fuck." I swung my door open hard, catching Warburton on the hip and jumped out after him. He spun to the ground and was on his back. Everything moved in slow motion. His arm was swinging up with his handgun ready as I lunged toward him—a race I had to win. I dove on him, my left arm swinging wide and knocking his shooting arm off target. I pulled my knee up and crushed his nuts at the same time. My chest hit him in the face, knocking his head into the pavement.

I lay there for a second, catching my breath. He was stunned, groaning and trying to get up. Baz came around the front of the car and stepped on Warburton's neck, applying what looked like almost too much pressure.

Almost.

I pushed myself to my feet and grabbed his gun from the road, and held it on him. "Okay, Baz. Let him up."

Baz gave him an extra little bit of pressure, then backed off. Warburton slowly stood.

"Hands out to your side. Go near the radio, and I'll shoot you in the knee."

"This is being recorded. You know that, right? There will be a recording of you attacking a police officer when you go to trial."

"This isn't going to trial, kid. You're going down with Grange. Where is he?"

Warburton stood in the middle of the road, hands out to his side. He looked at Baz and back at me. "You guys are so fucked."

Baz jumped forward, smacked Warburton on the back of the head and skipped back out of range. "We're the ones with the gun, idiot."

"Relax, Baz. I'm not going to shoot him. Take his radio and cuffs for me, will you?"

Baz sidled forward to the constable, grabbed Warburton's mic from his lapel and followed the cord down to the radio. It was firmly affixed to his belt.

"Can't get it, Mac."

I waved the gun at Warburton. "Take the belt off. All of it."

"Fuck you."

Baz unleashed an elbow to the side of Warburton's head, knocking him to the ground. I stood over him with the gun. "Quickly, or I'll let him hit you a few more times.

Warburton clenched his jaw and fumbled with the buckle. "So, so fucked. When Grange is finished with—"

I kicked him in the nuts again. He talked too much.

Baz finished removing his belt and tossed it to me. I caught it. "Help him into the driver's seat of the Toyota, Baz."

I held the gun on him while I awkwardly removed the cuffs from the back of his belt. I needed an extra hand. Finally extracted them and tossed them to Baz. "Lock his hands through the steering wheel. Make sure you take the keys out of the ignition."

Baz was giggling like a school kid. He squeezed the cuffs tight. Tossed me the car keys. I dropped the belt, caught the keys and threw them into the marsh on the side of the road.

I walked up to Warburton and pressed the gun into his thigh. "Where's Grange going? Don't worry, I'll miss the artery, but you'll be off active duty for the rest of your life."

He clenched the wheel hard enough to bend it. "You don't have the balls."

I cocked the gun.

"He's heading to Sal's to get reinforcements."

"There can't be many left."

"Enough. And they're really pissed off at you."

I released the hammer and slid the gun into my belt, in the back, under my shirt. I leaned down, carefully avoiding a knee to the face, and popped the hood release. "Help me out here, Baz. We need to disconnect the battery so this young man doesn't lay on the horn when we leave."

"We have time for that?"

"We can't *not* do it. Check the boot. Find a spanner or crowbar and destroy the battery, at the very least."

"You gonna help?"

"I'm going to sit here and make sure our cop pal doesn't get any stupid ideas."

Baz grunted and opened the boot. I heard the clatter of tools, raising my confidence that this would be sorted quickly. Baz barked out a laugh and ran to the front of the car.

"What did you get?"

He grunted and metal squealed and he grunted again and the dashboard lights went off. I leaned in and pressed the horn. Nothing.

I slammed the door shut, closed the boot and walked to the front. Baz had used a crowbar to lever one of the battery posts off the battery. Acid spilled down the side of the housing. It was an environmental mess, but mice nuts compared to the damage the local coal mines did.

I clapped him on the back and closed the hood. "Good man. Ever ride the front seat of a police car?"

"Can you drop me somewhere? Anywhere. I don't want to come up against Grange. Don't get on well with the cops." He gestured at Warburton. "This ain't gonna help any."

I nodded and got in the cop car. "Hop in. I

need to pass The Pelican to get to Sal's. I'll drop you there."

The front seat of the police car was crowded. Radio, radar, what looked like a radar detector detector, camera, GPS, radio and enough switches to keep a pilot happy. And keys in the ignition, engine running.

Baz squeezed into the passenger's seat. "Home, James."

Warburton had shit in his car that we hadn't even dreamed of when I was on the force. I poked around the touch screen, trying to delete the video Warburton would have taken while pulling us over. Unsuccessfully.

Baz clipped his seatbelt. "We're in bigger shit for this than slugging boy-o, you know that, right?"

I gave up on the computer, pulled the car into gear and floored it. My head snapped into the headrest. "No choice, Baz. Hold on. This thing has more guts than anything I've driven since I retired."

"I heard you were marched out."

"Whatever." The car handled well enough. I kept the red and blues flashing, just because. I tossed my phone to Baz. "Find Steve in this thing and call him, will you? Put it on speaker."

I managed rapidly approaching corners and intersections while Baz played with the phone. He must have found it because I turned to ask him what was taking so long and the phone was in my face, ringing just starting.

"Steve here. Mac, what's the plan?"

"I need to borrow your car."

"Yours is parked just across the road. Take it."

"I need something fast. I'm dropping Baz off in a minute at your end and need to be at Sal's immediately after."

"What's wrong with what you're driving?"

I looked at the GPS and other assorted stuff in the car. "It's hot."

"Yeah, but you can drop it back off at Sal's. Nobody will be the wiser."

"I don't have that one anymore. Just get your car ready, okay?"

I nodded at Baz, and he hung up the phone.

I coasted into The Pelican parking lot and fumbled around on the dash, trying to turn off the blue and reds. I flicked the siren on for a brief, sphincter-puckering second before I found the lights switch.

"We gotta wipe our prints off this, Mac, or we're doing hard time."

I laughed. "Dinner's on me, Baz. Eat it out here, though, okay? You're pretty rank. Thanks for all the help."

Steve and Gerry ran out the front of The Pelican and stopped when they saw Baz and I getting out of the cop car.

"Gerry, Baz gets whatever he wants off the menu. On me. Okay?"

Baz yawned. "I'll sit out here on the patio, though, so as not to disturb your other customers." He dragged a chair away from a table and slouched in it. "Can I get a menu?"

Gerry and Steve stood, gaping. Steve snapped out of it first. "What in the hell?"

"Had to disable a Grange crony."

"You killed a cop?" Gerry was a nice guy but not the fastest car on the track.

"Jesus, no. Warburton pulled us over and tried to kill Baz. Between the two of us we subdued him and cuffed him to the steering wheel of the Toyota I took from Sal's place. Where Grange is heading now, if he's not already there. I've got to disable him while I can before more muscle shows up."

Steve headed toward his car. "I'll come with you." I followed, not at all unhappy to have him along.

Baz turned in his chair. "Don't forget to grab the kite bag while you're there. Might be some evidence you can use."

I stopped. "What?" I turned to look at Baz, who was poring over a menu. "Baz, what the fuck are you talking about?"

He looked up. "Huh? There was a kite bag behind the dumpster. I saw it when I came to. Those boys don't look like kite surfers to me. Seems like it might have been Jessie's."

I ran to the car. "Gerry, ANYthing he wants."

Steve had it to the floor before I got my belt on. "You'd think Baz would have mentioned that before now."

I pressed against the door while I tried clipping myself in. "You don't know Baz that well. Christ only knows what else is in that head of his."

"So tell me about Grange. Why him?" He

down-shifted, hit a traffic circle and accelerated out of it.

"When I met Jackson and Grange at the beach, the day Jackson was killed, Grange copped part of the soda Jackson threw at me. When he changed his shirt," I tapped my shoulder. "blue-ringed octopus. Same as Sal's boys and the two surfer dudes. He was the cop inside, keeping Sal's crew out of jail as much as he could."

"You're guessing."

"Not about the tattoo. And not about his involvement. The kid I relieved the cop car from as much as confirmed it. So we're good to go."

Steve drove in silence, thinking all kinds of things I didn't want to have answers for. He looked at me, half smile on his face.

"So what did you do to the kid?"

"The cop? It was Warburton—the guy who marched me out of the hospital. Baz and I deweaponised him, disabled the Toyota I left him in and cuffed him to the steering wheel. We're getting close. Slow down. Is there enough light to run up with the headlights and running lights off?"

"Let's see." He turned off the lights and we were plunged into darkness. Streetlights were few and far between. He slowed, and we crept up the road. He stopped short of the garage. It was dark.

"We beat him here," said Steve. He turned off the ignition, and we eased out of the car. Slowly, we pressed the doors closed.

A streetlight halfway down the block cast very little light on the front of the shop. But I could see the dumpster Baz had collapsed beside, jammed against the wall. I motioned for Steve to hang back and keep an eye out. I pulled the dumpster from the wall and peered into the shadows. Couldn't see anything. I took out my phone and used the torch app, and the area was instantly flooded with way more light than it should have produced. I looked up, squinting. Floodlights on the outside of the garage were on. There were no shadows anywhere.

The bag was there, though. Clear as day. And it was the bag I carried off the beach.

Chapter Thirty-Five

The main garage door rolled up. Grange stood there with his arms crossed.

"Where's my man?"

"Warburton?" I bit the inside of my cheek to keep from smiling. "Last I saw him he was tied up. On Ruttleys."

"You kill him?"

"Jesus, Grange. What kind of guy do you think I am? I mean, I know what kind of guy *you* are. I still don't know why Jess. If you'd pinned Jackson's murder on almost anyone else, I wouldn't have batted an eye."

He shrugged, arms still crossed. "I didn't kill

Jackson."

"Fucking, hell. I'm not an idiot. I don't want this to be some stupid shoot-out or dragged-out fight. I've got you dead to rights."

"You've got nothing." He had a smug, stupid smile on his face.

"I used to like you, Grange. Kind of embarrassed to be wrong."

I saw Steve, in my peripheral vision, sliding back into the darkness, heading in the direction of his car.

I took out my phone. Sent a quick message and showed the phone to Grange. "I've got Dick admitting to it and Warburton telling me you instructed him to take me out." I put the phone in my pocket. "So why Jess? Was that your idea? Because it was a fucking stupid idea."

I reached behind me and pulled Warburton's gun from the small of my back. I pointed it in Grange's general direction.

Grange laughed. "What are you going to do with that? Arrest me? Take me off to the station and book me? Kill me? No, not that. You don't have the balls for that." He uncrossed his arms. He held *his* handgun, steady like a rock, aimed at my forehead. "I, on the other hand, do."

I dove to the left, putting the dumpster between him and me. Just in time. The shot whined off the corner of the steel box and spun off into the bush across the road.

"I said no shoot-out, Grange. It's stupid." I lay on the ground and peered around the bottom of the dumpster. Steve had scuttled out of sight, and Grange was bearing down on me. Warburton's gun was well out of reach between me and him.

"I thought Jess was a good touch, mate. She's young. No priors. Diminished capacity, what with her anger and all. Meeting you two at the beach was a lucky coincidence that set everything up perfectly. And if you think you'll get more than that out of me, you're nuts."

I'd wedged myself behind the dumpster. The kite bag was at my feet, mainly under the bin and out of sight.

I placed both hands on the side of the dumpster and took a deep breath. Shoved as hard as I could, like I was going to do a clap push-up, something

I hadn't done in over a decade.

The dumpster wheels screamed as it glanced off Grange. Not hard enough, unfortunately. Grange bounced sideways but stayed on his feet. He stepped around the corner, pointing his gun at my centre mass like a good cop.

"Stand up. I'm not going to kill you out here."

I used my foot to slide the kite bag under the dumpster as I raised my hands and stepped out. "Well, that's a relief. Where *will* you kill me?" I looked past him into the garage. It was empty of people. "In there would be worse for you. Too hard to explain. Impossible to clean all the trace. You know that. And where's your muscle?"

"Give me your phone." He waited for a minute, then smacked me on the side of the head. "Now."

I dug out my phone and handed it to him.

"You're going to get in my car. We're going for a drive."

"To the beach? You've got to be fucking kidding me. Do you have no imagination?"

He grunted and opened the passenger door of

his car. "You going to behave, or do I have to knock you out?"

If I ran, he'd shoot me. If I tried to take him on, one-on-one, he'd shoot me. Survive the next minute, and see what happens. I slid into the front seat. Not an unmarked police car. It was either his personal vehicle or one from the garage that he'd burn out after he was finished with it. I was guessing the latter—no point in throwing his own car away.

He held the gun on me as he walked around the front of the car and got in the driver's side. Held it on me as he started the car and put it into gear. Steady as a rock.

He *was* heading to the beach. That was obvious after the second turn.

"So what's it going to be? A mugging? Suicide?"

"Shut up."

I looked out the windscreen as we travelled up the Central Coast Highway, through the dark Magenta Park. "No, really. I want to know. Need to prepare myself." I looked at him. "You expecting me to write a suicide note?"

He said nothing.

"You know that for a *fact* you won't get away with this."

"Oh, for fuck's sake, of course I will. I'll make sure the investigation goes through me. I'll bury it so deep you won't even be a whisper in the wind in a month's time. Now shut the fuck up, or I'll make it painful." He turned into the parking lot.

"I'll be fucked if I'm going to make this easy for you." My seatbelt was off. I shoved the door open and rolled onto the pavement. A shot ploughed into the door, and it bounced closed.

The lot was dark, fortunately. I stayed low and ran for the dunes. I could hear Grange grunting somewhere behind me, but only fools look over their shoulder when a pissed-off man with a gun is chasing them.

I scrambled over the top of the grassy dunes and dropped into a depression on the beach's side. I sank low in the sand, trying to put together a plan. A slight onshore breeze brought with it the warm smell of the ocean. In other circumstances, it would have been a beautiful night for a walk on the beach.

It took me a couple of seconds before I realised that the depression I was in was Jackson's final resting place. Fitting.

Grange was quartering the dunes. I couldn't see him, but I could hear him stumbling through the sand. And when he was beach side, upwind of me, I could smell his cologne.

This was seriously anticlimactic. And I couldn't expect to stay in the sand much longer without getting found out. He was getting closer. I heard him stumble up the fucking planks. He was using the light from his phone to search. I waited until it swept away from me and lunged. I caught him near the top of the stairs, and we rolled down the planks toward the parking lot, grunting, cursing and farting like the two old men we were. I didn't see his gun, but something metallic clattered on the pavement.

He was bigger than me, but I think I was more pissed off. I drove a fist into his gut while I was on top of him. He grappled and rolled me over. He landed a couple of punches to my face before I got an arm free to cover myself. I pushed him off and rolled to my knees, looking for the gun.

I heard a click as he cocked it. "You looking for this? Get up on the beach. You know where."

"You're insane." I looked around the parking lot. Warburton's gun was about four metres away from me, too far out of reach. The best acting in the world couldn't find an excuse for me to get there.

"Look, I'll shoot you here if I have to, but I don't feel like dragging you up the steps to the rocks."

I ignored him. Took a short step toward the other gun. I don't think he knew it was there. He certainly wasn't acting like he knew.

"Mac, get the fuck over here." He took a step closer to me. A step farther away from the water.

I took another step in the general direction of the gun, and he shot me. I felt the bullet tear through my thigh. Searing pain dropped me to my knees. "Son of a bitch, you arsehole. How in the hell am I supposed to walk over the dunes with a shot leg?" I grabbed at my thigh and felt the hot, sticky blood seep through my fingers. Thank Christ it was seeping. He either was a great shot or lucked out, but he missed vital arteries. The pain throbbed, though, and I was getting really tired of being in pain. I rolled to my knees and stood, testing my leg. It hurt, but I could walk.

"Up the steps, Mac. Sorry." He got in behind me as I walked.

"You're not sorry at all. *I'm* sorry I was too stupid to figure this out earlier." I slowed my walk as I approached the plank steps. Grange was getting lax. A bit overconfident.

He got too close. I felt the barrel of his gun touch my back, just what I was waiting for. I spun hard to my left, my left arm extended. It knocked his gun hand—his right hand—out of the way as I followed through with my right elbow to his jaw. He dropped like a sack of sand. I picked his gun up off the ground and hobbled over to Warburton's and grabbed it, too. I got back to Grange, and I was ready to call it a night.

He stirred and opened his eyes. Blindly reached for his belt while kept his eyes on mine.

I waved both guns. "I've got both of them. Give me your phone."

He propped himself up on his elbows and looked at me. He rubbed his jaw and spat. He slowly reached into his pocket, took out his phone, and threw it into the parking lot. "Fetch."

I held one gun against his leg and levelled the other at his head. "I used to like you, Grange. I'd hate myself for killing you. But not too much." I thumbed the hammer back on the gun on his leg and pulled the trigger.

Grange let out a yell and fell back. It was much worse than what he did to me. I know I went through the femur. And there would be a lot more tissue damage. Fuck him.

I limped around the parking lot, looking for the phone. A seated throw limited the distance, and the direction was pretty fixed. It was hard to concentrate over the yelling, though. "Would you shut the fuck up, Grange? I'm trying to think."

About that time, I stepped on the phone. Heard the screen crack and almost fell over trying to get my foot off of it, putting all my weight on my shot leg. "Shit, motherfuck." I sat on the ground and peered at the phone. The display was honeycombed, and the phone was unusable. Shit.

I limped back to Grange. "Drag yourself to your car. We're going to have to drive out of here."

He didn't respond. He was still conscious, but

a bit woozy. I squatted down in front of him. "I sure as shit don't want to drag you, you fat fuck. But if I have to, I have to."

I got around behind him and grabbed him under his armpits. He was heavier than he looked— more muscle than fat. I had him halfway to his car when a pair of headlights turned into the parking lot.

Awkward. I started running stories through my head, trying to come up with one plausible enough to explain two shot legs.

The headlights stayed trained on us as the car slowly rolled to a stop a few metres away.

The car was an unmarked police car. The antennas were a dead giveaway. Both driver and passenger doors opened, and King and Steve got out of the car like they'd been rehearsing.

King removed her gun from its holster and trained it and a torch on me. "Mac, put down Grange and show me your hands."

I dropped him a little harder than I had to and placed my hands out wide from my body. "Lily, I can explain."

"I got your message. Went to the garage and

you weren't there. Steve thought you might end up here. He's smarter than he looks."

"Hey," said Steve. "Unnecessary."

King smiled. "So you want to explain why Senior Constable Grange is on the floor, bleeding from his leg and blubbering like a baby?"

"He started it." I lowered my hands. "You said you got my message."

"I got a sound file with Dick admitting to killing Jessie and your location. Nothing about Grange." Her gun was lowering, but it was still on me.

"Jessie's kite bag is under the dumpster outside Sal's garage. Best get someone there fast before one of her boys finds it." I slowly eased down beside Grange and ripped open his shirt, exposing his shoulder. "This tatt. Same on all of Sal's boys, including the surfer dudes. When Jackson killed the two surfers, he became a target. Grange coordinated it."

Grange looked up at King. "He's full of shit. I don't know what he's talking about. Arrest him."

"Hang on a minute, King. Did you find Warburton's car?"

"Why would I be looking for it?"

I laughed. "Jesus, you guys. His car is outside The Pelican. He's not with it. He's cuffed to a piece of shit Toyota I took from Sally's garage."

"What?" She raised her gun again. "What are you saying?"

I put out both hands to placate her. Steve was sliding back into the car. "Hear me out. Warburton's car records all of his traffic stops, right?"

"Audio and video."

"There'll be a recording of him stopping me in that crappy Toyota, trying to shoot Baz and then admitting that Grange ordered it. Take me in until you see the recording, if you want, but lock Grange up, too."

She holstered her gun and pressed her lapel mic. "I need an ambulance to the Budgewoi Beach parking lot. Make it fast. We have an injured officer."

She walked over to Grange and poked his leg with her toe. "Is what he said true, Willy?"

He fell back onto the parking lot and closed his eyes. "Jackson had to go. Fucking Mac should have kept his nose out of it. Everything would have been fine."

Chapter Thirty-Six

Good news: Jess was cleared pretty quickly. Bad news: I had to testify in court. Charges were filed against me for stealing Warburton's car and forcibly confining him, but they were dropped once all of the evidence was made known. It made for an interesting few days.

And a busy few days.

When I was clear of that, I took Ernie out to Betty's bolt hole and sat down with them.

"Ernie, Betty deserves better than you, but she loves you. I'm going to leave you here. Talk it out. Make a decision. I'm not going to be covering for either of you again."

"Covering?" asked Betty. "What do you mean?"

Shit. I looked at Ernie and shook my head. "You better tell her, pal. I've got things to do. Loose ends to tie up."

I limped back to my car. Steve was in the passenger's seat.

"They okay?"

I shrugged. "For a year or so I was playing one off against the other. Betty would hire me to catch Ernie cheating on her, and Ernie would pay me to cover his ass. I have a feeling that's going to come out shortly. Best not be anywhere near this place when that happens."

I pulled out of the drive and pointed my way back to The Pelican. "So, how long are you going to hang around?"

"I'm heading back soon. But I'll make sure you get to the premier, okay?"

"I don't get into Sydney often."

"We'll have it up here. Only fair. Let's head back to The Pelican. I'm hungry."

Fifteen minutes of easy driving got us to the parking lot. "I'll join you in a minute."

I made my way across the street and up the stairs. Sophie was reading a book, sitting across from my desk. A fresh cup of tea sat on a table beside her. "Join me for lunch?" I smiled. She didn't. Still a bit of strain between us, but we were working it out. "Steve's buying."

She sighed, looked at me, stuck a bookmark in her book and poured her tea down the sink. "Okay. Let's go."

Steve held court in a corner booth. Jessie and her parents were also at the table. Sophie and I joined them, one of us at either end of the crowd. Still a little frosty.

"Glad you could join us, Soph. I was telling Jessie and her folks that when we premier the movie next year, we're going to do it up here. I want all of you to attend. My guests. Jessie, if you'd do me the honour, I'd like you to be my plus one."

ABOUT THE AUTHOR

Tony McFadden is a Canadian now happily living in Australia, a land with very little snow, writing near the beach whenever possible.

You can find him on the interwebs at www.TonyMcFadden.net, Twitter (@Tony_McFadden), and Facebook (Writings on the Beach). Stop by and say hi.

Also by Tony McFadden

Matt's War
Daly Battles: The Fall of PyongYang
Target: Australia

G'Day LA
G'Day USA

Book 'Em
Family Matters
Unprotected Sax
(with Charles McFadden)

Have Wormhole, Will Travel
Killing Time

Mac D: Private Investigator
A Step Too Far (A Mac-D Mystery)
Hunter / Prey (A Mac D Mystery)

The Murder of Jeremy Brookes
Number Fifteen

Batteries Not Included
Broken
Dead Tomorrow
Under the Shadows